Retold by **Victoria Spence**

Activities by **Kenneth Brodey, Robert Hill**

Illustrated by **Ivan Canu**

Editors: Emma Berridge, Robert Hill
Design and art direction: Nadia Maestri
Computer graphics: Tiziana Pesce
Picture research: Laura Lagomarsino

New edition

Picture credits:
© The British Museum: 4, 9-10, 44, 54, 83; By Permission of the British Library, London: 5; Musée de la Tapisserie, Bayeux, France, With special authorisation of the city of Bayeux /Giraudon/ The Bridgeman Art Library: 7; NEW LINE CINEMA/THE SAUL ZAENTZ COMPANY/ WINGNUT FILM/Album: 42; WARNER BROTHERS/ Album: 73; Lessing Archive: 84.

We would be happy to receive your comments and suggestions, and give you any other information concerning our material.

www.blackcat-cideb.com

ISBN 978-88-530-0636-3 Book + CD

Printed in Italy by Litoprint, Genoa

Contents

The Historical Background 4
The Cultural Background 9

CHAPTER **ONE** 14
CHAPTER **TWO** 25
CHAPTER **THREE** 35
CHAPTER **FOUR** 48
CHAPTER **FIVE** 57
CHAPTER **SIX** 66
CHAPTER **SEVEN** 75
CHAPTER **EIGHT** 88
CHAPTER **NINE** 96
CHAPTER **TEN** 103

Dossiers The Heroic Elements in *Beowulf* 44
What Makes an Epic 83
Christian Elements in *Beowulf* 86

ACTIVITIES 8, 11, 20, 30, 41, 46, 53, 61, 70, 79, 84, 87, 92, 100, 107

EXIT TEST 108

INTERNET PROJECT 112

KEY TO THE **EXIT TEST** 112

First Certificate in English Examination-style exercises

T: GRADE 7 Trinity-style exercises (Grade 7)

This story is recorded in full.

These symbols indicate the beginning and end of the extracts linked to the listening activities.

The Historical *Background*

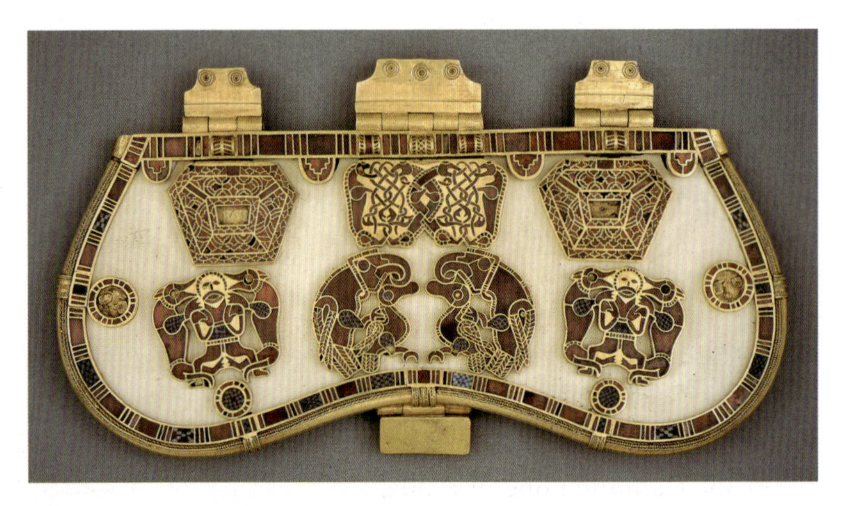

Purse lid (early 7th century) from the Anglo-Saxon treasure found at **Sutton Hoo** in eastern England.

In the fourth century, the Roman Empire in western Europe began to break up. The Roman army left Britain in 410 and the Celtic people, who the Romans conquered [1] and who then adapted to life under the Roman Empire, could not govern the country on their own. In the fifth century the Anglo-Saxons began to invade [2] Britain. These invaders came from north Germany and Denmark, and included different peoples: the most important were the Angles (the word 'English' comes from this name), the Saxons and the Jutes.

1. **conquered** : took complete control of.
2. **invade** : enter by force, with soldiers.

The Celtic people were forced to move to the north and the west, where they kept their language and culture in Wales and Cornwall. Although many examples of Celtic art survive, none of their literature remains.

By the seventh century, the Angles had established kingdoms in the east, north and centre of England, the Saxons had established kingdoms in the south and south-west, and there was a Jutish kingdom in the south-east. Eventually, they were united in the early ninth century under the kingdom of Wessex (the West Saxons).

The Anglo-Saxons were pagans [1], and in 597 the Catholic Pope in Rome, Gregory, sent a priest called Augustine to Britain to convert [2] them to Christianity. Augustine became the first Archbishop of Canterbury [3], and within a hundred years the Anglo-Saxons had converted to Christianity, although pagan ideas did not disappear completely.

A page from the **Lindisfarne Gospels** (early 8th century), an illustrated bible made in an Anglo-Saxon monastery on Lindisfarne island, north-east England.

1. **pagan** : pagan religions are older than the main religions of the world. Pagans believe in many gods, and nature is important for them.
2. **convert** : persuade someone to change their religion.
3. **Archbishop of Canterbury** : the head priest of the Anglican Church, the most important person in the Christian community in Britain.

At the end of the eighth century the Vikings, fierce people from Norway and Denmark, began to carry out raids [1] on the British coast. The raids soon became invasions, and Vikings began to live permanently in parts of Britain. Alfred the Great, king of Wessex from 871 to 899, was the only king who successfully resisted them.

Alfred fought many battles against the Danes (the name that was now given to the Viking invaders) and founded [2] the first English navy. He also encouraged the development of English culture, and had some important Latin works translated into Old English (the name given to the language of the Anglo-Saxons).

Despite Alfred's successes, eventually a Danish king, Cnut, became king of England in 1017. Anglo-Saxon rule started again in 1042, but it did not last long.

A statue of **King Alfred the Great** by the modern British sculptor Andrew du Mont.

1. **raids** : sudden violent attacks.
2. **founded** : started or built for the first time.

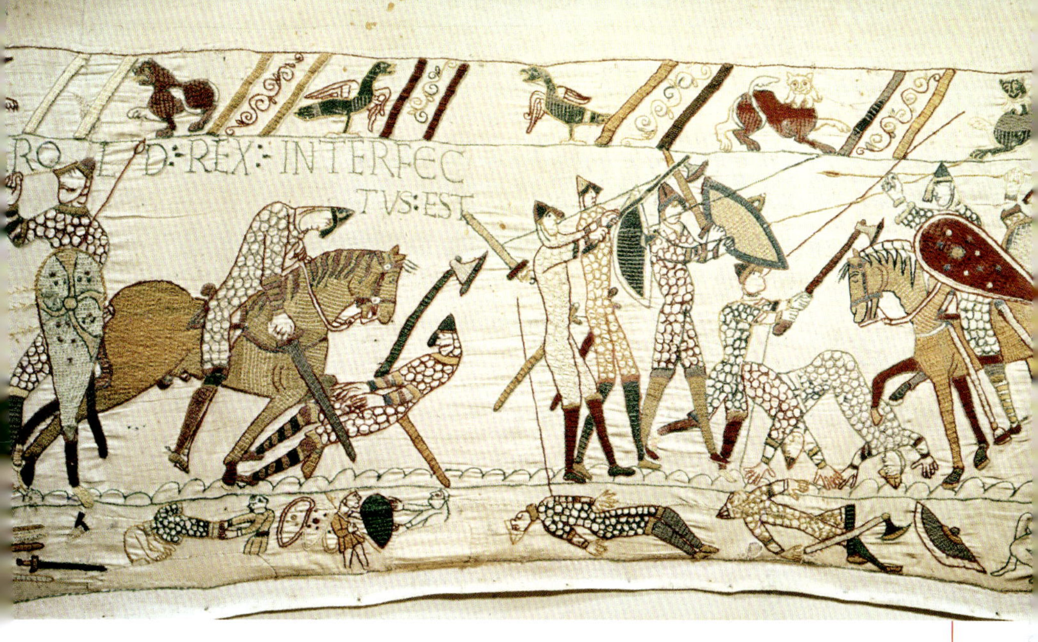

Harold, the last Anglo-Saxon king of England, is killed at the Battle of Hastings in 1066. Detail from the **Bayeux Tapestry** (about 1070-92).

In 1066, the Anglo-Saxon King Harold was defeated by William, leader of the Normans, a people descended from [1] the Vikings who went to live in Normandy in north-west France. After this – the last invasion of England – William became King William I of England. Nowadays, you will often hear people refer to the English-speaking peoples of the United Kingdom, the Commonwealth and the USA as 'Anglo-Saxons'. This term is inaccurate, however: in the British Isles, the Irish, Scots and Welsh are mostly descended from the Celts and the Vikings, while in the USA fewer than 15% of the people are descended from the British.

1. **descended from** : related to people who were born a long time before.

1 Comprehension check

Say if the following statements are True (T) or False (F). Then correct the false ones.

		T	F
1	After the Romans left Britain the Celts formed an effective government on their own.	☐	☐
2	The Anglo-Saxons were just one people.	☐	☐
3	Celtic culture survived in some parts of Britain.	☐	☐
4	Augustine, the first Archbishop of Canterbury, was sent to England by Pope Gregory.	☐	☐
5	When Christianity was introduced into England, pagan ways disappeared immediately.	☐	☐
6	Alfred the Great was the only king who managed to resist the Danes.	☐	☐
7	A Dane was king of England for a short time.	☐	☐
8	The Normans, who conquered England in 1066, were also Anglo-Saxons.	☐	☐

2 Northmen

The word 'Normans' comes from 'Northmen'. They arrived in Normandy in 911, converted to Christianity and adopted the French language, but remained violent and restless. The 'Norman Conquest' of England in 1066 is their most famous expansion out of Normandy, but soon after this other Normans founded kingdoms in the south of Italy and Sicily.
Do some research on the Normans, and find out how they expanded out of Normandy and what happened to them.

The Cultural *Background*

Beowulf, a poem of 3,182 lines, is the longest surviving poem in Old English. It is also the first important example of poetry in a European language that is not Greek or Latin, and is the only complete example of Germanic folk epic that exists.

A few historical references in *Beowulf* are from the sixth century, but the version of the poem that we have now was probably composed between 700 and 750. We do not know the name of the author, but it is thought that it was composed by just one person. Like other early poetry, *Beowulf* was first told orally and passed on from poet to poet over a long time before finally being written down. In Beowulf there are some references to the Anglo-Saxon poet – called scop (pronounced 'shop') in Old English – who gave oral performances of poems, usually by singing them, on special occasions. The first written version of *Beowulf*

The first page of the manuscript of *Beowulf*, written in Old English.

Gold belt buckle (early 7th century), from the Anglo-Saxon treasure found at **Sutton Hoo** in eastern England.

is a manuscript [1] from about 1000, which can now be seen in the British Museum in London.

The events of the poem are set in southern Scandinavia, and are mostly a mixture of Germanic myth and legend, although there are a few historical references. The main values of the poem are loyalty to chief and tribe and revenge [2] on enemies, although there are also some comments from a Christian point of view.

Beowulf, like nearly all Germanic and Old English poetry, uses alliteration. This means that the sounds of consonants – especially at the beginning of words – are repeated in words that are near to each other: e.g. *They put his **b**ody on the **b**oat and then **b**egan to **b**urn it.*

English poetry only started to use rhyme – in which the last syllables of words have the same sounds – after the Norman invasion of 1066, when French styles of poetry were introduced into England.

1. **manuscript** : an old example of a book or piece of writing, written by hand.
2. **revenge** : to do something to hurt people who have hurt you.

1 Comprehension check

Make notes below to make a fact file about *Beowulf*.

1 Three reasons why it is famous.

   a It is the longest surviving poem in Old English.

   b ....

   c ....

2 When it was composed.

....

3 Why it was not written down at first.

....

4 When it was written down.

....

5 Name of the poet.

....

6 Where the events are set.

....

7 Main values found in the poem.

....

8 Most important element of style.

....

9 Where the manuscript is kept now.

....

2 A poem from your culture

Make a similar fact file about an important poem in your culture. Then use your fact file to make a presentation of the poem you have chosen.

Before you read

1 Anglo-Saxon warriors and weapons

Match the words with the pictures.

shield spear knife helmet axe sword armour hilt

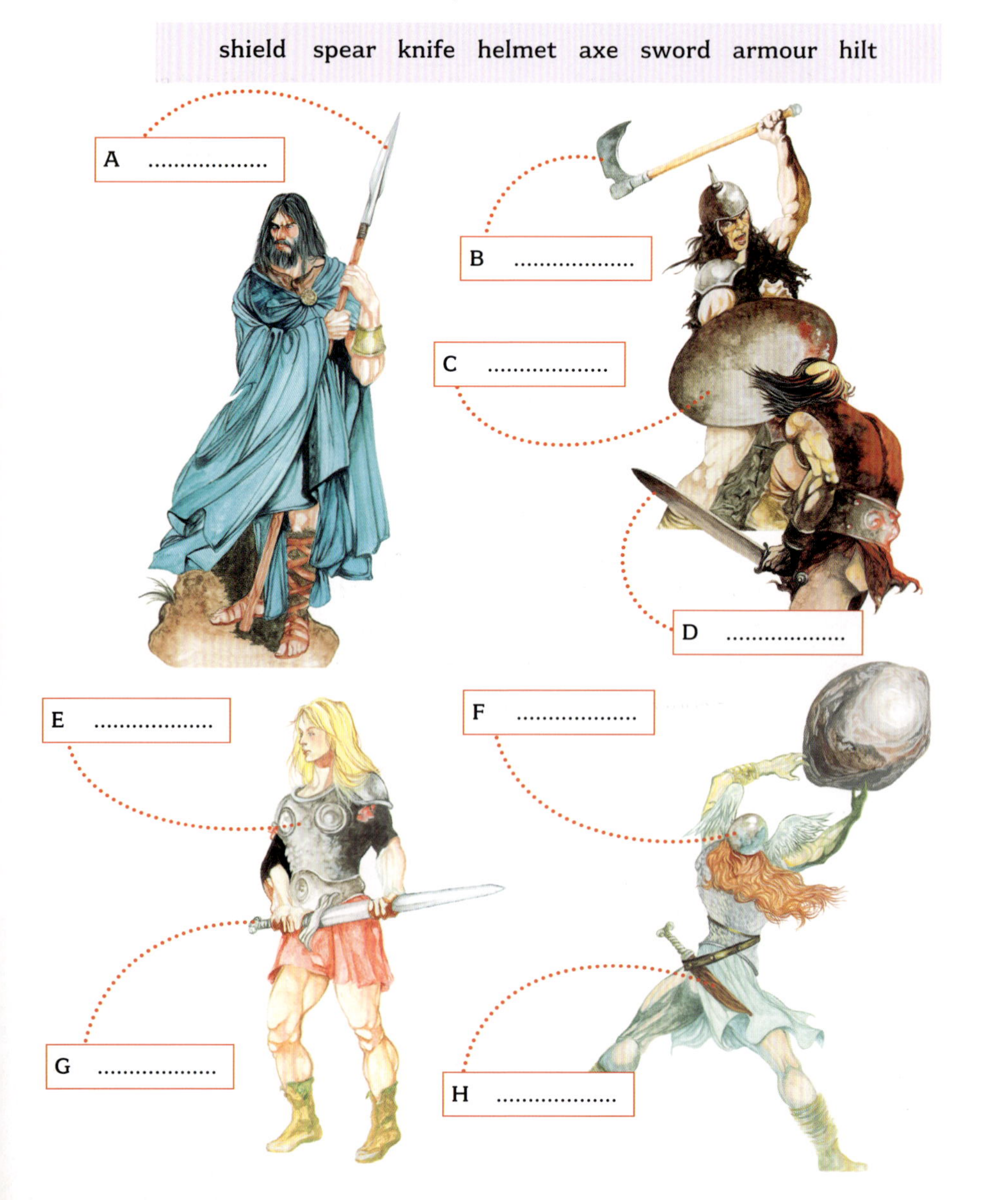

2 Reading pictures

In two minutes, look through the illustrations in this book. How many of the weapons named on page 12 can you find?

3 Anglo-Saxon kings and customs

On the first two pages of this story you are going to read about some elements of life at a royal court in sixth century Denmark. Make your predictions from the choices below, then read and/or listen to Chapter One to find out if you were right!

1 The place where the king has his court is known as
- A ☐ the Palace.
- B ☐ the Castle.
- C ☐ the Hall.

2 To show his royal authority the king sits on
- A ☐ shields that have been taken from enemies in battle.
- B ☐ cushions of precious material taken during raids.
- C ☐ a decorated, impressive chair called a throne.

3 The drink that people drink when they celebrate is
- A ☐ mead, an alcoholic drink made from honey and water.
- B ☐ strong, dark beer, served in big, decorated metal cups.
- C ☐ cider, an alcoholic drink made from apple juice.

4 The music at court is usually played on the
- A ☐ harp.
- B ☐ lute.
- C ☐ flute.

The old Danish kings were men of courage, and their exploits [1] are famous.

One of these kings was called Shield Sheafson. He had been abandoned as a child, but he grew into a fierce warrior who subdued [2] his enemies. He was a good king.

Shield Sheafson's son was called Beow. Beow recognised what the people had suffered in the past, and he rewarded them generously whilst his father was still king. In this way the young prince, who was blessed [3] by God, gathered around him friends who would be loyal in times of trouble.

When Shield died, he was given a splendid funeral. They placed his body in a boat and loaded the boat with treasure. They hung a golden standard [4] above his head to show who he was. Then they pushed the boat out to sea, where it drifted [5] on the waves. No one knows who found the boat and kept its rich treasure.

Now it was Beow's turn to protect the Danes. He, too, was a good king and the people liked him. Beow's heir [6] was the great Halfdane. Halfdane had three sons, Heorogar, Hrothgar and Halga.

1. **exploits** : adventures.
2. **subdued** : conquered.
3. **blessed** : helped and protected.
4. **golden standard** : gold-coloured flag.
5. **drifted** : was carried by the movement of the water.
6. **heir** [eə] : someone who receives a person's property when they die.

He also had a daughter who married the Swedish king Onela.

Hrothgar was lucky in war. Many men were keen to serve him and his army grew. He decided to build a great mead hall as a sign of his power. He wanted the mead hall to be his throne room. He also wanted it to be the place from where he would share his goods with the people.

He summoned [1] workers from all over the world to come and build his mead hall, which was called Heorot Hall. Soon the building was finished, and it was splendid. Its towers rose high into the sky, and its roof was wide.

There were feasts and singing every day in Heorot Hall. Harpists [2] played their music, and poets told the story of how God created the earth, the sun and the moon.

But there was a demon [3] that hated the happiness of Heorot Hall. His name was Grendel, and he lived on a bleak [4] part of the coastal lands. Grendel had previously lived in exile with the family of Cain, who had murdered his brother Abel. [5]

One night Grendel came to Heorot Hall to look at the Danes feasting and enjoying themselves there. He found them asleep after their drinking, and he seized [6] thirty men and carried them away with him. He returned to the Hall later that night, and left thirty bloodstained [7] corpses [8] there.

1. **summoned** : ordered to come.
2. **harpists** : musicians who play the harp.
3. **demon** : evil spirit.
4. **bleak** [bli:k] : empty and unpleasant.
5. **Cain and Abel** : the sons of Adam and Eve, who in the Bible are the first people on Earth.
6. **seized** : took hold of violently.
7. **bloodstained** : covered in blood.
8. **corpses** : dead bodies.

Beowulf

When morning came the Danes woke up and saw the bodies of their friends. They wept[1] at the sight. King Hrothgar did not know what to do, and he was ashamed[2] that he had not been able to prevent the terrible deed.[3] He was sad for the loss of his men.

The next night Grendel came back again, and killed more of Hrothgar's men. The Danes were now afraid, and they began to leave Heorot Hall.

Grendel now ruled. Heorot Hall was abandoned. King Hrothgar suffered for twelve long years. Musicians carried the story of Grendel all over the world. They sang about the horrible murders, and the long war between the demon and the king. They sang about the danger that everyone felt.

Grendel continued his attacks on the Danes. He took over Heorot Hall, although he could not enter the throne room.

King Hrothgar's advisers made plans to defend the kingdom from the demon. Sometimes, too, they prayed to false gods for help in their trouble. They forgot the real God who made the heavens and the earth.

The king of Geatland[4] was called Hygelac. One of his lords had heard about the demon, and he decided to help Hrothgar. This lord was the strongest man on earth, a real warrior. He gave orders that a boat should be made ready for him to travel in. He found fourteen men who were willing to go with him, and they set off together in his boat.

The lord's boat sailed quickly through the waves on its

1. **wept** : cried.
2. **ashamed** : sorry and embarrassed.
3. **deed** : event, action.
4. **Geatland** : the Geats were from the south of Sweden.

journey. They soon reached their destination, and they were glad to be on land again. They thanked God for the swift crossing.

When the Danish watchman saw men in armour come out of the boat, he went to them and issued a challenge: [1]

'Who are you, and why have you come here in armour? My job is to watch for the arrival of dangerous men on our shores. [2] I have never seen a group of armed men like you before. You did not ask anyone for permission to land.'

The watchman looked at the warrior, and then he went on:

'And I have never seen a man as big as you. You must be an important man. You must tell me who you are, before you go inland from the coast. And you must also tell me why you have come here.'

The warrior gave this reply to the watchman:

'We are from Geatland, and our king is Hygelac. I am the son of Ecgtheow, who was a great soldier in his day. We have come here to help your king, and we have no secret purpose. Therefore, please tell us what has been happening here. We want to know everything about this great danger that comes in the night, this killer of men in your country. I want to offer Hrothgar my help and advice. I know how to defeat this enemy, and how to make the king calm again.'

The watchman looked at the warrior, and then he replied:

'I believe you. Pick up your armour and your weapons, and I'll take you to the king. My men will look after your boat until you go back to Geatland.'

1. **issued a challenge** : ordered them to reply to questions.
2. **shores** : beaches, coast.

The text and **beyond**

1 A family tree

Complete this family tree of the Danish kings.

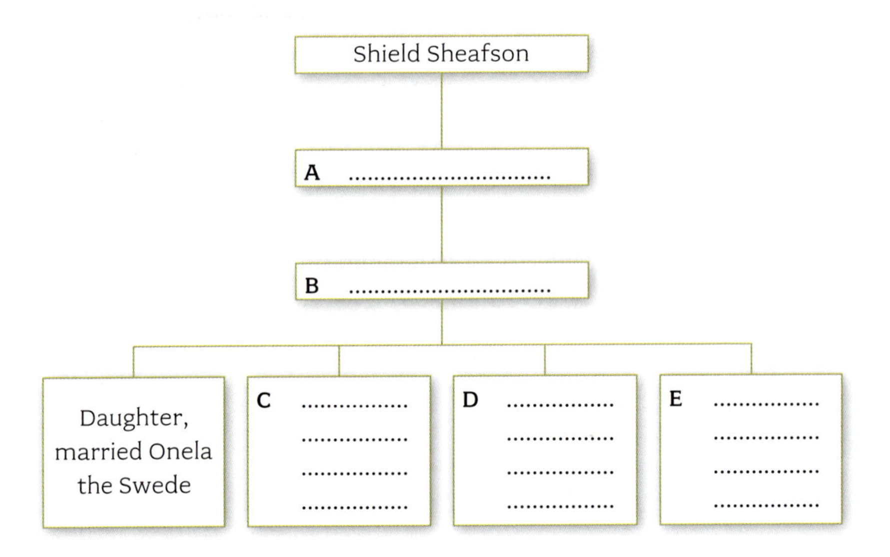

2 Comprehension check

Answer the following questions.

1 Why did Hrothgar want to build a mead hall?
2 What was the name of Hrothgar's mead hall?
3 What did Hrothgar's musicians sing about?
4 Who was Grendel?
5 What did Grendel do?
6 Why was Hrothgar ashamed?
7 How did the strongest man on earth hear about Grendel?
8 What did the strongest man on earth do when he heard about Grendel?

'I have never seen a man as big as you'

The Present Perfect Simple (1)

The Present Perfect Simple (subject + *have/has* + past participle) has a number of uses in English. One of the most common is when we want to talk about a period of time that began in the past and continues up to the present.

For example, the watchman says, *'I **have** never **seen** a man as big as you.'* He means that in his entire life (a period of time which began in the past, i.e. when he was born) he has never until now seen such a big man before.

Often, but not always, we use the adverb '**never**' when the period of time is our life. The adverb '**ever**' is used for questions.

*I have **never** been to Denmark (in my life).*
*Have you **ever** been to Denmark?*

If we want to make a positive statement regarding some unspecified time in our lives, we can use just the Present Perfect Simple without an adverb.

*I **have been** to Denmark* (some time in my life).

3 The Present Perfect Simple

A Use the ideas below to make sentences with *never* and questions with *ever*.

Example: they/fight/dragon?
Have they ever fought a dragon?

1 Beowulf/tell/a lie.
2 you/read/a book about the Vikings?
3 Beowulf/run away from a battle.
4 I/see/an Anglo-Saxon historical site.
5 Susan/see/Denmark?
6 You/meet/someone from Scandinavia?
7 They/see/the film of *Beowulf*?
8 Tom/use/a sword?

The Present Perfect Simple with **'ever'** is also often used with the superlative.

*You are **the biggest** man I have **ever** seen.*

B Transform the following into sentences with the superlative.

Example: I have never fought a warrior as strong as Beowulf.
Beowulf is the strongest warrior I have ever fought.

1 She has never read a story as exciting as *Beowulf*.
2 Beowulf has never fought an enemy as dangerous as Grendel.
3 I have never seen a king as sad as Hrothgar.
4 Beowulf has never seen a hall as magnificent as Heorot.
5 We have never seen a country as beautiful as Sweden.
6 They have never studied a language as hard as Old English.

4 Speaking

In pairs or groups, use the words from the table to ask and answer questions. Then tell the class any interesting information you have found out about each other.

What Who is the	most boring most exciting best most interesting most expensive worst funniest most frightening etc.	person film book holiday place meal story concert thing etc.	had read seen met bought heard been to etc.

Example: 'What's the most exciting holiday you've ever had?'
'In Sweden. Three years ago. Fabulous natural scenery!'

Before you read

FCE

1 Fill in the gaps

Decide which word (A, B, C or D) best fits each space. Then listen to the recording and check your answers.

The watchman (**1**) .... the Geat soldiers to Heorot Hall. They were amazed when they saw the huge (**2**) .... Now the watchman (**3**) .... them, saying that he had to go back to his duty on the coast. The Geat warriors approached the Hall. Their armour shone in the sun (**4**) .... they walked. When they entered the building, they sat in the Hall.
The Danes were curious (**5**) .... the newcomers, and asked them questions: 'Who are you, and why have you (**6**) .... here carrying your weapons?'
The Geat warrior (**7**) .... this answer:
'We are Hygelac's men. Beowulf is my name. I will (**8**) .... your king the purpose of our visit if he will see me.'
A Wendel chief called Wulfgar agreed to take Beowulf's message to the king. He said that a group of people from Geatland had come ashore, led by a warrior called Beowulf, (**9**) .... seemed a strong man. Hrothgar replied:
'I know Beowulf. I remember him (**10**) .... a young boy. They say he has the strength of thirty men. God has sent him here to defend us against Grendel.'

1	**A** showed	**B** carried	**C** led	**D** aimed
2	**A** building	**B** construct	**C** fabrication	**D** facility
3	**A** abandoned	**B** deserted	**C** left	**D** departed
4	**A** like	**B** meanwhile	**C** as	**D** when
5	**A** about	**B** of	**C** from	**D** for
6	**A** arrived	**B** got	**C** reached	**D** come
7	**A** gave	**B** answered	**C** replied	**D** said
8	**A** say	**B** communicate	**C** report	**D** tell
9	**A** which	**B** whose	**C** who	**D** whom
10	**A** when	**B** like	**C** well	**D** as

2 What happens next?

When Beowulf and his warriors go into the throne room, Beowulf introduces himself and speaks to the king. Which of the following do you think he says? He says five of them; the other five are wrong. Put a tick (✓) in the boxes, compare your ideas in class, and then check your predictions on page 26.

		YES	NO
1	After saying his name, the very first thing Beowulf says to the King Hrothgar is that he (Beowulf) has had great victories against his (Beowulf's) enemies.	☐	☐
2	After saying his name, the very first thing Beowulf says to the King Hrothgar is that he (Beowulf) will obey the king at all times.	☐	☐
3	Beowulf says that he has never forgiven anyone who has in any way harmed his own people, the Geats.	☐	☐
4	Beowulf says that he has sometimes forgiven people who have harmed his own people, the Geats, if they were noble.	☐	☐
5	Beowulf asks the king for seven brave Danish men to fight Grendel with him.	☐	☐
6	Beowulf asks the king to let him fight Grendel alone.	☐	☐
7	Beowulf says that courage will decide who wins the fight against Grendel.	☐	☐
8	Beowulf says that God will decide who wins the fight against Grendel.	☐	☐
9	Beowulf asks King Hrothgar to send his armour back to his father if he is killed in the fight.	☐	☐
10	Beowulf asks King Hrothgar ask his father to come to Denmark if he is killed in the fight.	☐	☐

CHAPTER TWO

3 **The watchman led the Geat soldiers to Heorot Hall.** They were amazed when they saw the huge building. Now the watchman left them, saying that he had to go back to his duty on the coast.

The Geat warriors approached the Hall. Their armour shone [1] in the sun as they walked. When they entered the building, they sat in the Hall.

The Danes were curious about the newcomers, and asked them questions:

'Who are you, and why have you come here carrying your weapons?'

The Geat warrior gave this answer:

'We are Hygelac's men. Beowulf is my name. I will tell your king the purpose of our visit if he will see me.'

A Wendel [2] chief called Wulfgar agreed to take Beowulf's message to the king. He said that a group of people from Geatland had come ashore, [3] led by a warrior called Beowulf, who seemed a strong man.

Hrothgar replied:

'I know Beowulf. I remember him as a young boy. They say he

1. **shone** : (*shine, shone, shone*) had a bright light
2. **Wendel** : the Wendels were a Germanic tribe who lived in North Denmark, where Beowulf lands.
3. **ashore** : onto the land.

has the strength of thirty men. God has sent him here to defend us against Grendel. I'll give him a large reward. Now go and ask the Geats to come in, and be sure to tell them they are welcome in Denmark.'

The Geat warriors went into the throne room, and Beowulf spoke to the king:

'I am Beowulf. I have had great victories against my enemies, and now I have heard the story of Grendel and the destruction he has brought to Denmark. Travellers have told us how Heorot Hall has been abandoned by its people because they are afraid of the demon. Hygelac's advisers encouraged me to come here to help you, because they know how strong I am. They know I have fought against men and sea-monsters, and have always avenged [1] the Geats. I want to fight Grendel in single combat. [2] I ask you to let me fight him like that. I have also heard that Grendel does not use any weapons. I won't use any weapons, either. We will fight with our hands only. God will decide who wins. I know that it will be terrible if Grendel wins. The demon will eat my body, and I won't have a proper burial. Then he'll kill my soldiers. If I die, please send this armour of mine back to King Hygelac. That's all I ask.'

Now King Hrothgar replied to Beowulf:

'You have come here to help us and to fight for us. I remember your father well, and how I helped him once when his people drove him away because of a feud. [3] I am sorry to ask anyone for help in our troubles with Grendel, but he is destroying my soldiers. Only

1. **avenged** : done something to hurt people who have hurt the Geats.
2. **single combat** : one against one.
3. **feud** [fju:d]: an argument, often violent, that lasts for a very long time.

God can stop him! Our men discuss the demon when they are drinking, and they promise to protect Heorot Hall. Often they have waited for him in the night with their swords. But in the morning their blood is found everywhere in the Hall. That's how they have died, and I have lost many soldiers.'

Hrothgar invited the Geats to dine in the Hall, and they sat together. They ate well, and a minstrel [1] sang for them.

One man was not happy that the Geats had come to Denmark. This was Unferth. He was jealous of Beowulf's courage and his fame. Now he spoke challengingly to the Geat warrior:

'Are you the same Beowulf who had a famous swimming match against Breca? That was just vanity [2]; you wanted to win even though people warned you of the danger. You went into the water and it was cold and rough. You struggled [3] for seven nights, but Breca was stronger than you. He reached the land one morning, and proved that he was a better swimmer than you. It will be the same with Grendel. No one has lasted an entire night against that demon.'

Now Beowulf smiled at Unferth as he answered him:

'That swimming match came about [4] because we had drunk a lot. What really happened was this. Breca and I were good friends. We had known each other all our lives, and we were always challenging each other. Both of us swam with a sword, to protect ourselves from the sea-monsters. I was stronger than him, and

1. **minstrel** : musician and singer; he usually sang about heroic events from the past. He is the same as the *scop* described on page 9.
2. **vanity** : being too proud.
3. **struggled** : tried very hard to win.
4. **came about** : happened.

could always swim further out to sea than he could. We went on for five days in that dreadful [1] cold, swimming side by side. Then the wind drove us apart. [2] Sea-monsters attacked me all the time, but I killed nine of them with my sword. In the end I landed safely.'

Beowulf stared hard into Unferth's eyes, and then he continued:

'I can't remember any struggle of yours like that, Unferth. You've killed your own people, [3] and so you'll go to Hell when you die. Anyway, if you were really as brave as you say, you would have done something about Grendel. But he knows that he needn't be afraid of you – or any Dane, come to that. But he'll soon learn that I am different. I'll show him what a Geat can do in battle. Heorot Hall will then be safe for you Danes again.'

King Hrothgar listened to Beowulf's words with pleasure. He relied on [4] the hero's courage and strength.

Now the noise of talking and happy laughter filled the Hall. Queen Wealhtheow entered. She greeted everyone and offered the king something to drink. Then she went round the Hall offering everyone a drink, as the custom was. When she came to Beowulf, she welcomed him to Denmark. She told him that God had answered her prayer by sending him. Beowulf took the cup from the queen, and replied to her words:

'I had a clear intention when I got into my boat with my men. That intention was to help your people or to die in battle with Grendel. I shall be true to that intention.'

1. **dreadful** : terrible.
2. **drove us apart** : separated us.
3. **own people** : Unferth has killed his own brother in a fight.
4. **relied on** : trusted.

The text and **beyond**

FCE **1** **Comprehension check**

Choose the right answer, A, B, C or D.

1 What is the mysterious warrior's name?
- A ☐ Geat
- B ☐ Hygelac
- C ☐ Beowulf
- D ☐ Wulfgar

2 What will Beowulf use to fight Grendel?
- A ☐ his sword
- B ☐ his knife
- C ☐ magic
- D ☐ his hands

3 Why won't Beowulf have a proper burial if Grendel wins the battle?
- A ☐ because Grendel will eat his body
- B ☐ because Beowulf will be dead in a foreign land
- C ☐ because the people are afraid of Grendel
- D ☐ because Grendel will kill Beowulf's soldiers

4 Why does Hrothgar remember Beowulf's father?
- A ☐ because they fought together as young men
- B ☐ because Hrothgar helped Beowulf's father when he was driven away by his people
- C ☐ because Beowulf's father helped Hrothgar when he was driven away by his people
- D ☐ because Hrothgar heard many stories of his great strength

5 Who was Breca?
- A ☐ Beowulf's enemy
- B ☐ Unferth's enemy
- C ☐ Beowulf's friend
- D ☐ the king of the Geats

6 Why did Beowulf carry a sword during the swimming match?
- A ☐ to protect himself against Unferth
- B ☐ to protect himself against Breca
- C ☐ to protect himself against the cold
- D ☐ to protect himself against the sea-monsters

2 Kennings & alliteration

The main characteristic of Old English poetry — and old Scandinavian poetry — is alliteration (see page 10). Another characteristic is a special kind of metaphor called a 'kenning'. The Scandinavian word 'kenning' is used for a metaphorical phrase, made up of several words, which replaces a noun. An example is a kenning for the sun: 'jewel of the sky'. Kennings are used a lot in *Beowulf* to add colourful descriptions to the story.
But sometimes the meaning is not easy for modern readers. For example, the kenning for a chief or king is a 'breaker of the rings'. This kenning comes from a king's custom of breaking off pieces of gold from spiral rings (which he often wore on his arm) to give as rewards to his followers.

Match the kennings in column A with the nouns in column B.

A KENNINGS	B NOUNS
1 ☐ the guardian of the kingdom of heaven	A sea
2 ☐ candle of the sky	B the human body
3 ☐ killer of souls	C sword
4 ☐ whale road	D sun
5 ☐ house of bone	E God
6 ☐ weaver[1] of peace	F ship
7 ☐ sea wood	G wife
8 ☐ light of the battle	H the devil

3 In pairs or small groups, make up modern kennings for some of the following:

best friend computer mother/father music mobile phone television car bed MP3 player something chosen by you

1. **weaver** : someone who makes cloth.

4 Anglo-Saxon alphabets

Read the passage about the alphabets used by the Anglo-Saxons, and then discuss the questions which follow.

The Goths, a Germanic people from northern Europe, adapted the Etruscan and Roman alphabets to create the runic alphabet, which was used in Scandinavia from the 3rd century onwards. The Anglo-Saxons then brought this alphabet to Britain.

The letters, called 'runes', were formed with straight lines so that they could be cut into stone, wood or bone. The earliest runic alphabet had 24 letters, but extra ones were added later. (You can see runes used around some of the pictures in this book; so far, they have been used on pages 16-17 and 27.)

The Christians who came to Britain to convert the Anglo-Saxons brought the Roman alphabet with them. They added some letters to represent Anglo-Saxon sounds that did not exist in Latin: for example *uu*, which later became *w*. The manuscript on page 9 is written in the Old English alphabet. But even if this alphabet is more recognisable than runes, Old English is very, very different from modern English: for example, the first word in the manuscript means 'Listen!'.

The Old English word 'rune' meant 'secret' or 'mystery', and runes continued to be used on monuments and in charms until the 17th century. Even today you can find runes used as magical decorations.

- Where does the alphabet that you use for your language come from?
- What are the famous early examples of documents in your alphabet?
- Do you know any other alphabets?

'You have come here to help us and to fight for us'

The Present Perfect Simple (2)

You looked at one use of the Present Perfect Simple on page 21. Another use is to make a connection between a past action and the present, to show that the action is relevant now.

Look at these sentences.

The watchman says, *'Why **have** you **come** here carrying your weapons?'*

Connection with the present: 'I am concerned about the safety of my country'.

Hrothgar says, *'God **has sent** him here to defend us against Grendel.'*

Connection with the present: I hope that now we will be saved from Grendel's attacks.

5 The Present Perfect Simple

For 1-6, write a second sentence so that it has a similar meaning to the first sentence. Put the verb given in the Present Perfect Simple.

Examples: I don't know how this book ends. (*read*)
I haven't read the whole book

We don't know your name. (*tell*)
You haven't told us your name

1 I don't think I know you. (*meet*)

....

2 I'm so sorry. I can't remember your address. (*forget*)

....

3 There's no-one here any more. (*go home*)

....

4 He doesn't have any money. (*spend*)

....

5 Brrr! Isn't it cold now? (*sun/go down*)

....

6 Lisa's a mother again! (*have baby*)

....

Before you read

1 Reading pictures

In pairs or small groups, look at the picture on pages 38-9. Describe what you can see. What do you think has happened? Compare your ideas in class.

2 Listening

Listen to Chapter Three and say whether the following sentences are true (T) or false (F). Then read the text and correct the false ones.

		T	F
1	The Danes were happy that Beowulf had arrived to fight Grendel.		
2	Beowulf did not use any weapons in his battle with Grendel.		
3	Everyone thought Beowulf would defeat Grendel.		
4	Beowulf thought that God would help him to defeat Grendel.		
5	Beowulf's men wounded Grendel with their swords.		
6	Grendel pulled Beowulf's arm and shoulder off.		
7	In the end, Grendel ran away from the Hall.		
8	One of the king's minstrels compared Beowulf with the great dragon-killer Sigemund.		
9	According to Beowulf, God will judge Grendel in the end.		
10	Unferth criticised Beowulf for not killing Grendel in the Hall.		

CHAPTER THREE

4

1 **There was a new atmosphere of cheerfulness [1] and hope in Heorot Hall now that Beowulf was there.** The drinking and laughter continued until it was time for Hrothgar and his queen to leave the Hall.

Hrothgar knew that Grendel would come that night, and he wished the hero good luck:

'This is the first time I have let anyone else defend Heorot Hall. Guard it well tonight, and be careful of the enemy.'

2 God had given the Danes someone who could protect them from the demon. Beowulf left his armour with a soldier, and told him to look after it well. Then he prepared for sleep, saying proudly:

'I will not use any weapons in the battle with Grendel. He is very strong, but with God's help I will overcome him.'

Beowulf lay down, and his Geats rested as well. No one expected that Beowulf would ever return to his own country, but God was preparing a victory for him. The Geats would win because of the strength of one man alone.

3 Suddenly Grendel came out of the darkness. He opened the iron door of the Hall and entered the great building. He was full

1. **cheerfulness** : being happy.

of hate. Once inside, Grendel moved secretly and quickly past the guards who were asleep. Grendel thought he would kill many men that night, but his days of murder were coming to an end.

Beowulf was watching the demon in the darkness. Suddenly the demon took hold of a man who was sleeping. He bit into [1] the man's body, and the blood flowed [2] everywhere. Then he moved towards Beowulf.

4 Beowulf leapt [3] up from his bed and began to wrestle [4] with the demon. The demon struggled against the warrior, but Beowulf held on to him tightly. Grendel tried to escape, but he could not free himself from Beowulf's grasp. [5] Man and demon were locked together in the fight, and the noise of their battle could be heard all over the Hall. Suddenly Grendel gave a great cry — it was the cry of the defeated. The man had beaten the demon.

5 Beowulf did not want to let Grendel leave the Hall alive. His men were awake now, and they rushed [6] to help their hero with their swords. They did not know that the demon could not be hurt by any sword. He had magic against human weapons.

Now Grendel began to weaken. Beowulf still held on to him, and the demon was in agony. [7] The injuries that Beowulf gave him were terrible. He pulled the demon's arm and shoulder off. At last the demon fled [8] the Hall. He disappeared into the

1. **bit into** : (*bite, bit, bit*) attacked, using his teeth.
2. **flowed** : came out, quickly and without stopping.
3 **leapt** : (*leap, leapt, leapt*) jumped.
4 **wrestle** : fight, using only hands, not weapons.
5 **grasp** : holding him with his hands.
6 **rushed** : moved quickly.
7 **agony** : great pain.
8 **fled** : (*flee, fled, fled*) ran away from.

darkness, but he was dying and he knew it.

6 The next morning warriors came from everywhere to discuss the battle. They saw the traces [1] of his blood on the ground outside the Hall. They saw the place where the demon had dived into the water and drowned. [2] His soul [3] had gone to Hell. The warriors praised Beowulf's courage. They said there was no braver man than him in the whole world.

One of the king's minstrels began to compose a poem in honour of the Geat warrior. The poet told the story of Sigemund the dragon-killer, and compared Beowulf to that hero.

7 King Hrothgar came into the hall with his queen Wealhtheow. He looked at the remains of Grendel's arm and shoulder, and then he spoke the following words:

'We must thank God for this victory. A little while ago, it seemed that this house would always run with the blood of Grendel's victims. But God brought Beowulf here, and Beowulf has achieved something that we Danes could not do.'

He turned and spoke directly to the Geat hero:

'I now think of you as if you were my son. I will give you all the wealth [4] that you want. I hope that God will always protect you and reward you.'

8 Now Beowulf replied to the king:

'We have survived this great adventure. I wish, all the same, that you could have seen his body here in the Hall. I wanted to

1. **traces** : marks.
2. **drowned** : died because he was under the water and couldn't breathe.
3. **soul** : spirit of a dead person.
4. **wealth** : riches.

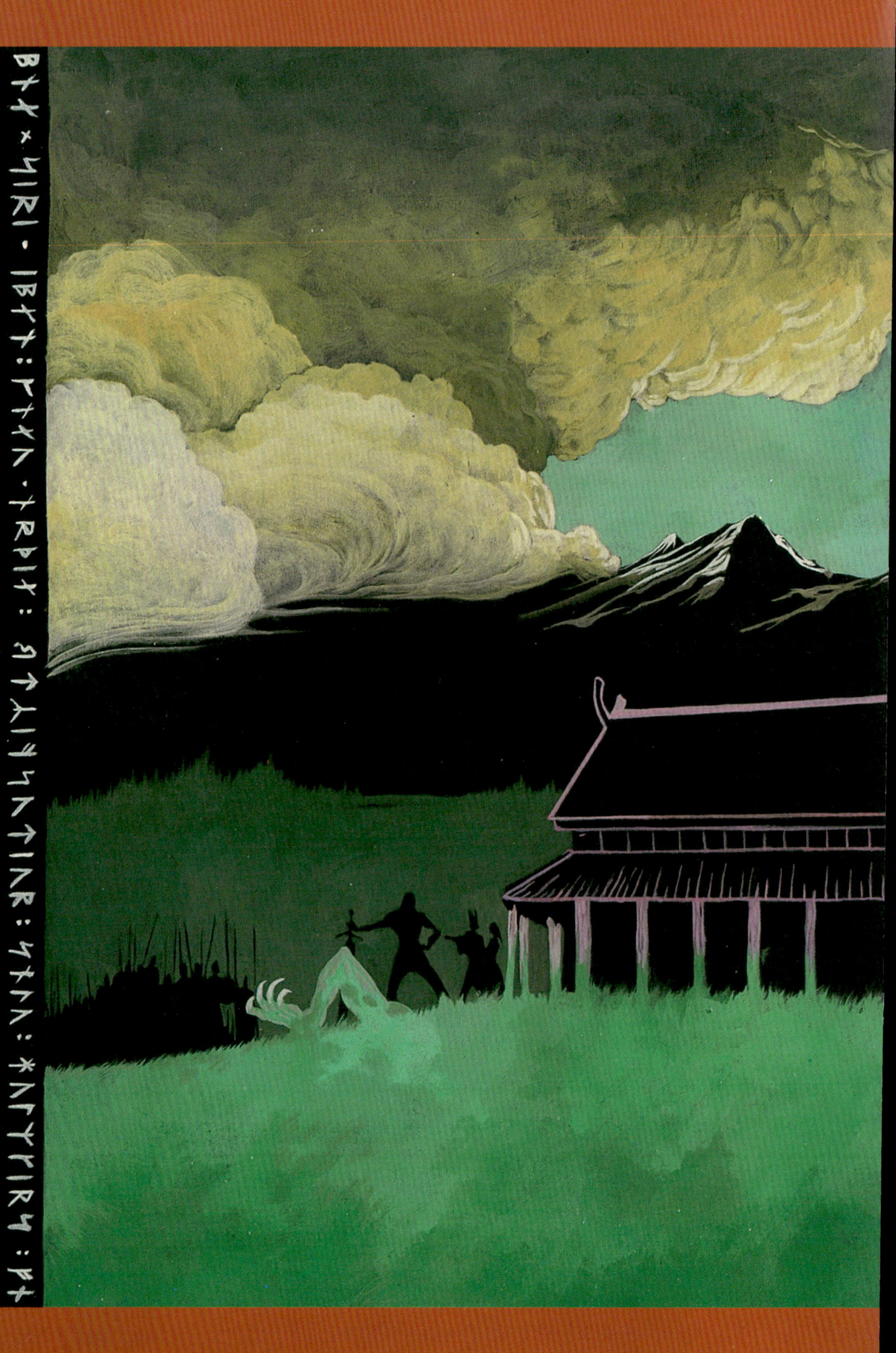

use my strength to make him fall down, and then to squeeze [1] the life out of him. He escaped me, however, and God allowed it to happen. The demon left his arm and shoulder here with me, and that was a heavy [2] price to pay for his freedom. He will soon be dead because of that injury, if he is not dead already. Then he will go before God and receive judgement for his wickedness.' [3]

Unferth looked at the demon's arm and shoulder, and he was quiet. He could not criticise Beowulf for anything now.

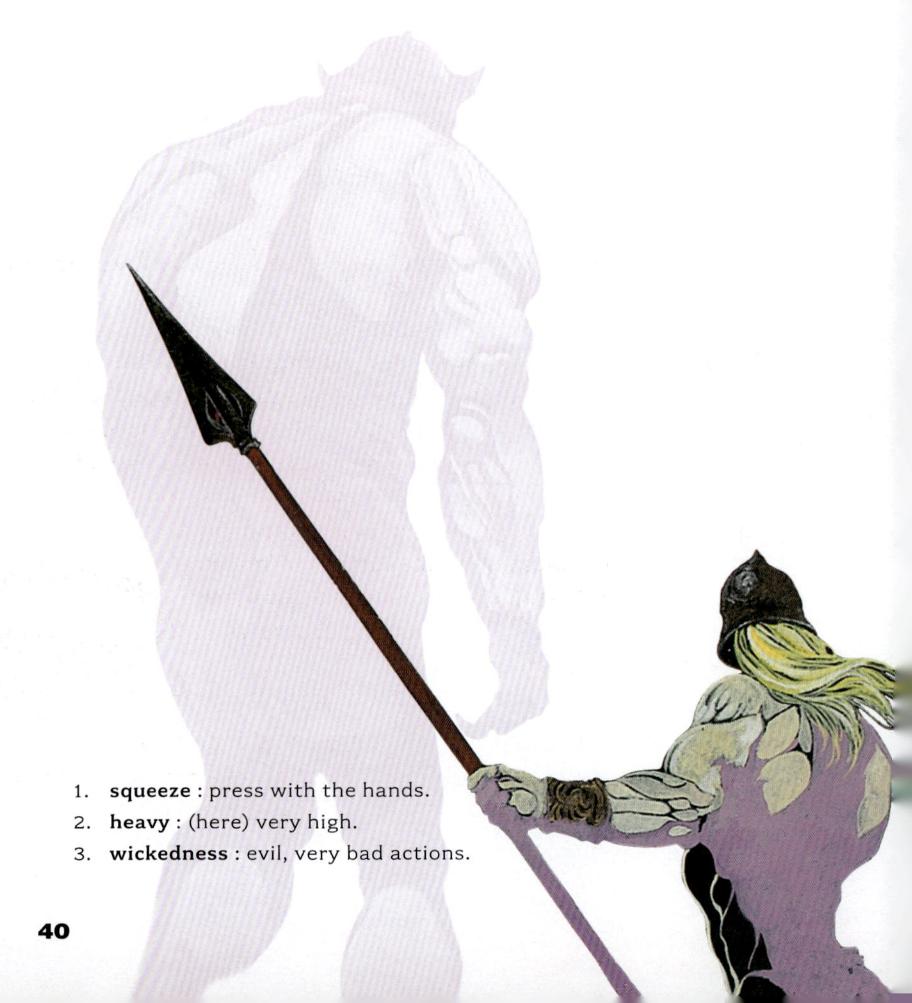

1. **squeeze** : press with the hands.
2. **heavy** : (here) very high.
3. **wickedness** : evil, very bad actions.

The text and **beyond**

1 Comprehension check

Chapter Three has been divided into eight parts. Choose the best title from the list A-I for each part (1-8). There is one extra title which you do not need to use.

A		The cry of defeat
B		He escaped, but not with his life
C		Unarmed against a demon
D		The celebration before the fight
E		Thank God for you
F		The murderer's last murder
G		A long hard journey
H		I sent him to God
I		Song for the victor

2 Kings, rings and dragons

Read about the life of this Beowulf expert, and then do the puzzle on page 43 to discover his name.

In one Anglo-Saxon poem about the Biblical creation, our world is referred to as the 'middangeard', or the Middle Earth; it is called this because our world is between the Heaven above and Hell below. In other Anglo-Saxon poems a king is referred to as the 'breaker of the rings' (see the 'kennings' on page 31) because he broke off a piece of gold from the rings he wore around his arms to give to his loyal followers. Nowadays, 'Middle Earth' and 'breaker of the rings' sound familiar after Peter Jackson's last film in his *The Lord of the Rings* trilogy won Oscars for best film and best director in 2003.

This is not surprising since the author of the books upon which the film was based, *The Lord of the Rings* trilogy, was a Professor at Oxford from 1925 to 1959. In particular, he studied Anglo-Saxon and Medieval literature, and in 1936 he published *Beowulf, the Monsters and the Critics.*

He was born in Bloemfontein in South Africa on 3 January 1892. When he was only four years old his father died and his mother took him and his brother back to England to live.

As a young man he served in the army during the First World War, and many men from his regiment were killed. The author himself was injured and during his stay in hospital he decided that what he wanted to do in his life was to study languages.

In 1919 he graduated from Oxford. He then taught for four years at the University of Leeds before going on to teach at Oxford. He always tried to make his lectures interesting, and his students liked him. One of his students even compared him to a hobbit, one of those friendly creatures made famous all over the world in his books.

He began the first of his famous novels, *The Hobbit* (1937), to illustrate his ideas about fairy tales, and *The Lord of the Rings* trilogy grew out of this book. The first volume, *The Fellowship of the Ring*, came out in 1954, and it was followed by *The Two Towers* and *The Return of the King*. The whole work took fourteen years to complete and it is filled with strange alphabets and names from and allusions to the Norse, Anglo-Saxon and Welsh languages.

These novels became immensely popular, so it is not surprising that the film industry decided to bring these stories to the screen. In fact, Peter Jackson's trilogy is not even the first film based on *The Lord of the Rings*. In 1978 an innovative cartoon version of the first volume and half of the second volume came out.

It is interesting to think how all this hi-tech entertainment comes from the fantasy world of a man who as a little boy 'desired dragons with a profound desire.' You never know where a reading of *Beowulf* will take you!

3 Vocabulary

This puzzle will tell you the last name of the author of *The Lord of the Rings*. Only look back to the pages given in brackets if you really need help.

1. Unferth was angry and upset because he knew that Beowulf was a braver and better warrior. Unferth was … of Beowulf (page 28).
2. A kind of a flag (page 14).
3. A musician and singer in Anglo-Saxon times (page 28).
4. Past tense of 'to leap' (page 36).
5. The preposition that comes after 'to rely' (page 29).
6. For the Anglo-Saxons it was essential that warriors were … to their king (page 14).
7. Very interested and enthusiastic (page 15).
8. The boat was carried by the movement of the water: it … (page 14).
9. Someone who receives a person's property when they die is an … (page 14).
10. To die under the water because you can't breathe is to … (page 37).

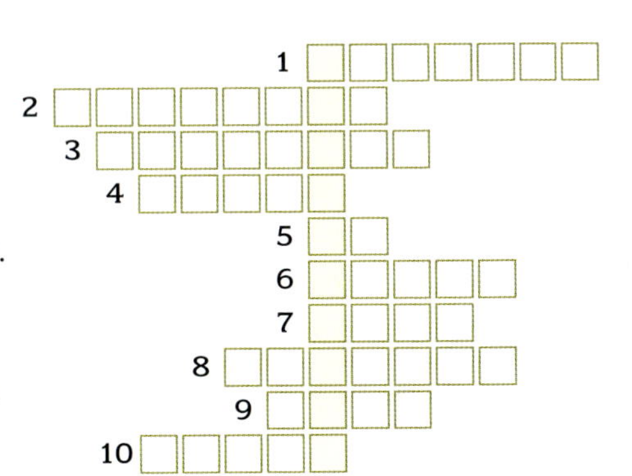

4 A review

If you have seen any of the films from *The Lord of the Rings* trilogy, prepare a short talk or write a review. Say what you liked and what you didn't like. Think about

- the story
- the characters and the actors who play them
- the action scenes
- special effects

The Heroic Elements in *Beowulf*

The world of *Beowulf* is made up of different kingdoms, ruled by warrior kings. So far, we have read about the kingdom of the Danes, ruled by Hrothgar, and the kingdom of the Geats, where Beowulf comes from, ruled by Hygelac. This king is mentioned by a French historian, Gregory of Tours, because he raided the Netherlands in 520; he is the only character in the poem that seems to be a real, historical figure.

The centre of each kingdom is the king's hall, where his followers come together, where guests are received, and where stories are told and heroic deeds are remembered in poetry and song.

The hall is full of warmth and light, human contact and laughter. In contrast, the outside world is a dark, dangerous place with thick, mysterious forests. The monsters in the poem belong to this frightening outside world, but they have the ability to invade the world of the humans. This shows the uncertainty and fear of the

An **iron helmet** with bronze decorations (early 7th century) from the Anglo-Saxon **Sutton Hoo** treasure.

pagan world. It is a world in which the unexpected – such as the sudden appearance of Grendel – plays an important part.

In *Beowulf* we can see all the qualities that the Anglo-Saxons thought a good king should have. Most of all, he must be courageous, a good fighter and a strong leader. He must also be honourable [1] and want to become famous. Another quality is the king's treatment of his people: he should be generous with gifts and reward those who serve him loyally. Finally, a good king must be wise: among other things, he must understand that human life does not last for ever, and he must accept that you cannot escape death. Accepting fate [2] is an important quality of a king.

Beowulf, who later in the poem will become a King of the Geats, has all these qualities. He is physically strong and courageous. He has become famous before he comes to Denmark to fight Grendel, especially because of the swimming match with Breca. He shows that he is honourable by refusing to use any weapons in the fight with Grendel, because he does not want to have any advantage over his opponent, but it is clear that he wants to become famous for having beaten Grendel. He thinks of his own men, and is generous to them. Finally, at the end of the poem, he accepts death without fear.

The values of the society described in *Beowulf* are mostly but not exclusively pagan: honour, the desire for fame, loyalty to chief and tribe, the importance of fighting and taking revenge on enemies. But this does not mean, however, that we should think that this society was primitive.

1. **honourable** : always doing what you believe is right, so that everybody thinks you are a good person.
2. **fate** : a power which some people believe controls everything that will happen, and which you cannot change.

1 Comprehension check

Look at the list of qualities below. Use your dictionary to help you if necessary. Nine of them – all mentioned in the text above – were heroic qualities in the early Anglo-Saxon world, qualities that a king should have. Five of them are not qualities appreciated in the early Anglo-Saxon world. Which are these five?

1. ☐ Sense of democracy
2. ☐ Generosity to one's own people or friends
3. ☐ Wisdom
4. ☐ Avoidance of violence
5. ☐ Sense of honour
6. ☐ Generosity to one's enemies
7. ☐ Desire for fame
8. ☐ Respect for other people's customs
9. ☐ Vengeance on one's enemies
10. ☐ Courage
11. ☐ Modesty
12. ☐ Strong leadership
13. ☐ Acceptance of fate
14. ☐ Skill in battle

2 Discussion

A **Think of a modern hero/heroine from fictional books, films or even computer games. (We can see a difference immediately: in Anglo-Saxon culture heroes were always male!) What qualities does he/she share with the Anglo-Saxon hero? What qualities are different?**

B **Think of someone from contemporary real life who is considered a hero/heroine. Does he/she share any qualities with the Anglo-Saxon hero, or the heroes you mentioned in A above?**

Before you read

FCE

1 Word formation

Do not look at pages 48-49. Read the text below. Use the word given in capitals at the end of each line to form a word that fits in the space in the same line. Then listen to the text and check your answers.

King Hrothgar ordered his men to prepare Heorot	
Hall for a (1) .... feast. Men and women	VICTOR
worked hard together to remove the traces of the	
(2) .... struggle between Grendel and	TERROR
Beowulf from the (3) .... Everything that	BUILD
had been damaged in the fight was renewed and soon	
the Hall looked splendid once more.	
On the night of the victory feast there was great	
(4) .... at Heorot Hall. The cup passed from	HAPPY
hand to hand, and there was happiness and	
(5) .... Hrothgar gave Beowulf a gold	FRIEND
standard as a victory gift. He also gave him some	
armour, a helmet, and a sword. Then the king told his	
men to bring eight horses into the Hall. One of the	
horses was wearing the king's own saddle. Hrothgar	
gave these horses to Beowulf as well.	
There were also rewards for the other Geats.	
Every man who had been on Beowulf's boat	
received a (6) .... gift, and there was	VALUE
(7) .... for the Geat warrior that Grendel	COMPENSATE
had killed. The harpists and (8) .... now	MUSIC
came forward, and they played tunes and sang tales	
of heroes to please the king and his guests. The poet	
recited a poem about an old feud between the	
Frisians and the Danes. The poem told a bitter story	
of blood, (9) .... and revenge. Everyone	BETRAY
listened to the recital with (10)	PLEASE

King Hrothgar ordered his men to prepare Heorot Hall for a victory feast. Men and women worked hard together to remove the traces [1] of the terrible struggle between Grendel and Beowulf from the building. Everything that had been damaged in the fight was renewed, and soon the Hall looked splendid once more.

On the night of the victory feast there was great happiness at Heorot Hall. The cup passed from hand to hand, and there was happiness and friendship.

Hrothgar gave Beowulf a gold standard as a victory gift. He also gave him some armour, a helmet, and a sword. Then the king told his men to bring eight horses into the Hall. One of the horses was wearing the king's own saddle. [2] Hrothgar gave these horses to Beowulf as well.

There were also rewards for the other Geats. Every man who had been on Beowulf's boat received a valuable gift, and there was compensation [3] for the Geat warrior that Grendel had killed.

The harpists and musicians now came forward, and they played tunes and sang tales of heroes to please the king and his

1. **traces** : signs.
2. **saddle** : seat that you put on a horse.
3. **compensation** : (here) money or something valuable given to Beowulf because he has lost a warrior.

guests. The poet recited a poem about an old feud between the Frisians [1] and the Danes. The poem told a bitter story of blood, betrayal, and revenge.

Everyone listened to the recital with pleasure.

Queen Wealhtheow said to Hrothgar:

'Drink to the Geats, my lord. Be generous to them, and enjoy their company. But think carefully about what you are doing. You have said that you think of Beowulf as if he were your son. Be sure you leave your kingdom to your own sons when you die. Remember your brother, Hrothulf. If you die before he does, he will look after Denmark for our children. He will treat them well.'

The queen glanced over [2] at her two sons, Hrethric and Hrothmund. Beowulf was sitting happily between the two brothers.

There were more gifts for Beowulf – gold, rings, and a magnificent torque. [3]

The queen spoke to Beowulf:

'Wear this torque for luck, and also this armour. I wish you luck throughout your life. Treat my sons kindly, because here in Denmark friends are loyal to each other.'

The feast continued. The warriors were drinking wine, and none of them knew the terrible things the future was bringing them. At last the feast came to an end, and guards were posted [4] at the Hall. Everyone prepared to sleep, but they kept their armour and their weapons close to them. That was the custom.

1. **Frisians** : people from Friesland (northern Germany and the northern Netherlands).
2. **glanced over** : looked quickly.
3. **torque** : kind of necklace (see page 54)
4. **posted** : put.

Beowulf

Beowulf was not in the Hall. He had been given a bedchamber away from the other warriors.

While everybody slept, something horrible entered the Hall in the darkness. Suddenly the Hall was full of noise and shouting, and the warriors woke up. There was a moment's confusion. People did not know what was happening.

Then they understood. Grendel's mother was determined to avenge her son's death. She had already killed one warrior while

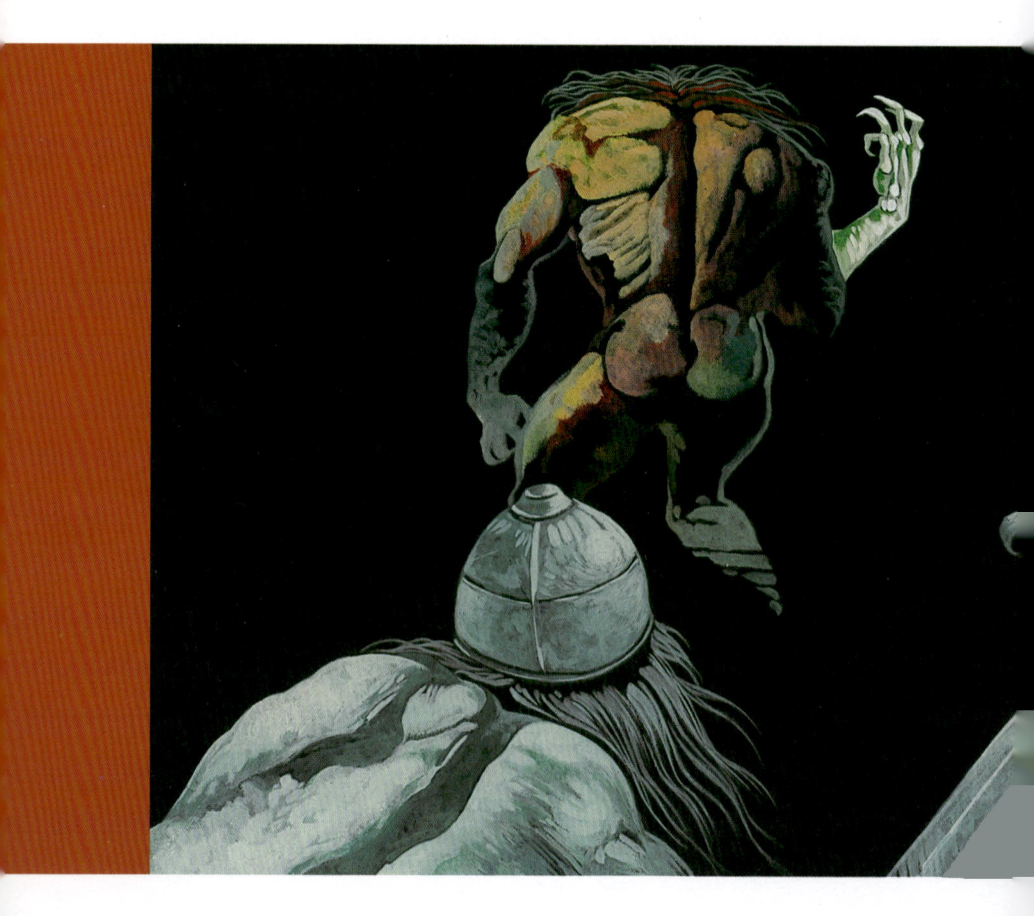

everybody was sleeping. She had taken the body to her hiding-place outside the Hall. The dead man was called Aeschere, and he had been one of the king's best friends.

The Danes reached for their swords as quickly as they could. Now the demon grabbed [1] her son's arm and shoulder and ran from the Hall.

1. **grabbed** : took violently.

In a few moments Beowulf came running into the Hall with his men. Hrothgar spoke to him:

'Suffering has come back. Aeschere is dead. He was my best friend, and always fought alongside [1] me in our battles. This monster came in and murdered him. She must have decided to avenge Grendel's death. I don't know where she is hiding, but I have heard some stories from some of the lords who live a long way from the Hall. They say that people saw two of these monsters. One of them looked like a man — that was Grendel, whom you killed. The other one looked like a woman — that must be his mother. There is a strange place a few miles from here where the forest comes down to a mere. [2] It is a forbidding [3] place because the water burns. An animal that is being hunted will turn to face the hounds [4] rather than dive into that water. You must go there, Beowulf, and see if you can find the demon.'

1. **alongside** : next to.
2. **mere** [miə] : small lake.
3. **forbidding** : extremely unpleasant.
4. **hounds** : dogs used for hunting.

The text and **beyond**

1 Comprehension check

Answer the following questions.

1 How did the Danes prepare Heorot for the victory feast?
2 What did the king give to Beowulf as victory gifts?
3 What was the poem which the poet recited about?
4 How does the king consider Beowulf after his victory over Grendel?
5 Why was the Queen worried?
6 Why did Grendel's mother come to the Hall?
7 What did Grendel look like?
8 What did Grendel's mother look like?

2 Anglo-Saxon values

Which of the heroic qualities of Anglo-Saxon culture (see the dossier on pages 44-46) do you notice most in Chapter Four?

3 Listening

***Beowulf* is told from the point of view of human beings. But what would we hear if it were told from the point of view of Grendel? Listen to the interview and choose the correct answer, A, B or C.**

1 Where does the journalist conduct the interview?
A ☐ at the Philadelphia Rock Club
B ☐ at Grendel's Lair
C ☐ at Cain's Bar and Grill

2 Why is the journalist surprised when he arrives at the club?
A ☐ because he can't see the owner
B ☐ because the club is famous
C ☐ because Grendel is very big

3 Who is the owner of the club?
A ☐ Grendel
B ☐ Mr Garfield
C ☐ Mr Kane

4 Why does Grendel agree to be interviewed?
A ☐ because he wants to be famous
B ☐ because he hates Beowulf
C ☐ because he wants people to know what really happened

5 What did Cain do after he killed his brother?
A ☐ He chased him from Eden.
B ☐ He became a monster.
C ☐ He drank his blood.

6 Why did Grendel begin attacking the Danes?
A ☐ because they didn't include him in their feasts
B ☐ because he hated Beowulf
C ☐ because he wanted to defend his mother

7 Which of the following was not one of Grendel's special powers?
A ☐ He could become invisible.
B ☐ He could change his body.
C ☐ He could do magical things with his eyes.

8 Why did the poets want to flatter Beowulf?
A ☐ because they wanted to get a special payment
B ☐ because they were afraid of him
C ☐ because they thought he was a great hero

4 Torques

Read the passage about torques and then discuss the questions that follow.

Queen Wealhtheow gives Beowulf a torque. This piece of jewellery is a stiff, circular necklace (or sometimes a bracelet), open-ended at the front. The word 'torque' comes from the Latin *torqueo* – to twist – because of the twisted shape of the collar.

Torques were worn in very early times, but are best known as necklaces worn by Celts in Britain, France and Spain. Celtic gods and goddesses are often shown wearing torques. The Anglo-Saxons wore torques, too, and a beautiful torque

Celtic gold torc

was found at Sutton Hoo (see page 100). Torques were a sign of high social status, and were often given as a prize to warriors who fought bravely.

The Roman consul Titus Manlius killed a Gaul (a Celt from France) in single combat, and took his torque. He always wore it, and so he was called Torquatus (the one who wears a torque). After this, the Romans adopted the torque as a decoration for brave soldiers.

The hippie movement of the 1960s and 1970s made torques fashionable again as necklaces and bracelets and also as rings.

What sort of jewellery do you like wearing? What do you know about the origin of this jewellery?

Before you read

1 Listening

Listen to Chapter Five and choose the right answers.

1 Beowulf told Hrothgar not to cry over Aeschere's death. Instead,
- **A** ☐ he should give him a splendid funeral.
- **B** ☐ he should avenge his death.
- **C** ☐ he should give a feast in his honour.

2 Hrothgar felt happier because
- **A** ☐ Beowulf told him that Grendel's mother could not escape.
- **B** ☐ he knew that a courageous king should not be sad.
- **C** ☐ Beowulf had killed Grendel.

3 What did Hrothgar and Beowulf find near the mere?
- **A** ☐ Aeschere's head
- **B** ☐ Grendel's arm and shoulder
- **C** ☐ Aeschere's sword

4 What did Beowulf see in the water?

A ☐ Grendel's mother
B ☐ monsters
C ☐ snakes

5 What was Unferth's gift to Beowulf?

A ☐ a helmet
B ☐ armour
C ☐ a sword

6 What did Unferth's gift prove?

A ☐ that Unferth was no longer angry with Beowulf
B ☐ that Unferth was rich
C ☐ that Unferth was afraid to kill the monster himself

7 How long did Beowulf swim before he saw the bottom of the mere?

A ☐ about an hour
B ☐ about three hours
C ☐ about a whole day

8 How did Beowulf manage to kill Grendel's mother?

A ☐ He struck her on the neck with her own sword.
B ☐ He struck her on the neck with Unferth's sword.
C ☐ He struck her on the head with her own sword.

CHAPTER FIVE

Beowulf replied to Hrothgar's words: 'Do not be sad, sir. It is better to avenge a friend's death than to cry over it. Let's go after this monster together. She won't escape, I promise you.'

Hrothgar was cheered [1] by Beowulf's words. He called for his horse immediately, and the king left the Hall with Beowulf and some warriors.

They rode into the forest, where they could see the tracks [2] of the monster. They followed the trail [3] until they came to the part of the forest where the mere was. Then they saw Aeschere's head lying on the ground in front of them.

The warriors looked around them. They saw monsters sitting on the cliffs [4] above them. Then they looked down at the water, and saw that it was full of snakes. Beowulf shot an arrow at one of the snakes, and they watched the horrible animal die in the water. Some of the warriors pulled the snake's body to the land.

Beowulf put on his armour. This would keep him safe from the monster when he fought it. He put on his helmet. Then he took a wonderful sword that had been given to him by Unferth. The

1. **cheered** : made happier.
2. **tracks** : marks left by the feet.
3. **trail** : line of marks left by the feet.
4. **cliffs** : very high rocks by the sea.

sword was called Hrunting. No one who used that sword had ever been defeated. Unferth's gift of the sword to Beowulf proved that he was afraid to pursue [1] the monster himself.

When he was ready Beowulf spoke to the king again:

'Remember what you promised me earlier, my lord. If I am killed in this battle, look after my men for me. And send the gifts you have given me to Hygelac. If I die, I want Unferth to have my own sword. The one he gave me I am taking with me to the battle.'

Then Beowulf dived into the foul [2] water. He swam down for nearly a whole day before he could see the bottom.

The monster was immediately aware that a human being was coming towards her. She swam up and caught hold of Beowulf. Then she dragged [3] the warrior down to the bottom. She took Beowulf to her court, holding on to him so tightly that he could not use his weapons against her.

When they arrived at the court Beowulf saw a great crowd of sea-monsters. They swam towards him and attacked him.

Beowulf sprang [4] free from the monster and raised his sword. He brought the sword down on the monster's head, but nothing happened. The magic sword failed him. [5] Beowulf threw it away in disgust. [6]

The warrior knew that he would have to fight the monster with his own strength. He seized her shoulder and threw her to

1. **pursue** : follow and try to catch.
2. **foul** [faʊl] : dirty and horrible.
3. **dragged** : pulled.
4. **sprang** : (*spring, sprang, sprung*) jumped.
5. **failed him** : didn't do what he wanted it to do.
6. **disgust** : anger and frustration.

the ground. Grendel's mother got up quickly and caught hold of him again. Beowulf lost his balance and fell. The monster jumped on top of him and pulled out a knife. She tried to stab [1] him, but Beowulf's armour was strong – it saved him from harm. [2]

Now God gave Beowulf the victory. He rose to his feet and grabbed a sword that he saw in the monster's armoury. It was a huge sword that no other man could lift. Beowulf picked it up and swung it [3] at Grendel's mother. The sword struck [4] her on the neck. She fell to the floor. Beowulf cut off her head.

1. **stab** : hurt him with a knife.
2. **harm** : hurt.
3. **swung it** : (*swing, swung, swung*) moved it quickly in order to hit something.
4. **struck** : (*strike, struck, struck*) hit.

The text and **beyond**

1 Summary

Put the sentences below (A-M) into the right order to make a summary of Chapter Five. The first and last sentences have been done for you.

A [1] The king was very sad because Grendel's mother had killed Aeschere, his best friend.

B [ ] He dived into the water and swam down for almost a day before he saw the bottom.

C [ ] When they got there, they saw Aeschere's head on the ground.

D [ ] When they got there, Beowulf escaped and hit her on the head with his sword.

E [ ] Hrothgar and Beowulf rode to the mere where Grendel's mother lived.

F [ ] Nothing happened so he had to fight her with his bare hands.

G [13] He grabbed it and cut off her head.

H [ ] She dragged him to her court.

I [ ] Then the monster stabbed Beowulf but his armour saved him.

J [ ] Beowulf put on his armour and took the sword which Unferth had given him.

K [ ] Beowulf told him that it was better for them to kill the monster than to cry.

L [ ] Grendel's mother saw him immediately and grabbed hold of him tightly.

M [ ] Fortunately Beowulf then saw one of the monster's great swords.

2 Speaking

Which of the events (A-M) in the activity above did you find the most surprising? Discuss this in pairs, explain the reasons for your choice, and then vote in class.

3 Film fights

Remember the different ways that Beowulf and Grendel's mother fight on pages 58-60.

1 Grendel's mother attacks Beowulf with her hands; they both fight with their hands.

2 Beowulf attacks Grendel's mother with his sword.

3 Beowulf throws his sword away, and attacks Grendel's mother with his hands.

4 They fight with their hands, then Grendel's mother attacks Beowulf with a knife.

5 Beowulf's armour saves him; he attacks Grendel's mother with a sword and kills her.

***Beowulf* is an old story, but fight scenes in modern films can be very similar! Characters often use different things – furniture, for example – after they can't use their weapons any more.**
In groups, think of fight scenes like this from films and tell the class about them. Better, bring a video or DVD of a fight scene to class, and give a commentary.
Fight scenes as in *Beowulf* or in films are not realistic, so why are they presented to the reader/film-viewer in this way?

'Beowulf cut off her head'

The Present Perfect Simple (3)

As we saw on page 33, the Present Perfect Simple can have something to do with the present. The Past Simple, on the other hand, tells us about things of the past, and it is the usual tense when we tell a story. For example:

*The sword **struck** her on the neck. She **fell** to the floor. Beowulf **cut** off her head.*

With the Past Simple we can use expressions that refer to finished time, such as *two days ago, when he was a child, last spring, in 1991* and questions with **when**: this is not possible with the Present Perfect Simple (***When** did you arrive?* not ~~*When have you arrived?*~~). With the

Present Perfect Simple we can use expressions that refer to unfinished time, such as *today, this week, this year*.

Now look at the sentences below.

Present Perfect Simple	Past Simple
*I **have read** two chapters of Beowulf today.* (It's lunchtime; the day isn't finished. Perhaps I'll read some more.)	*I **read** two chapters of Beowulf yesterday.* (Yesterday is finished.)
*She **has** never **been** to a concert in Central Park.* (Never in her whole life.)	*She never **went** to a concert in Central Park.* (When she lived in New York. Now she lives in Rome.)
*Philip **has lived** in London for ten years.* (He still lives in London.)	*Jamie **lived** in London for ten years.* (She doesn't live there now.)

4 The Present Perfect Simple

Put the verbs in brackets in the Past Simple or the Present Perfect Simple according to the context. There is an example at the beginning (0).

0 When I was a young man, I (*have*) ....had........ a swimming contest with Breca and I (*win*) ....won........ .

1 Beowulf said, 'Hrothgar, you look frightened. What (*happen*) ....?' Hrothgar replied, 'Grendel's mother (*murder*) .... my best friend.'

2 Immediately after killing Grendel, Beowulf said to Hrothgar, 'When I was a young man I (*kill*) .... many monsters, but Grendel is the fiercest monster I (*ever/kill*) ....'

3 A minstrel sings, 'Then Beowulf (*kill*) .... Grendel; in all my life I (*never/hear*) .... of a greater warrior.'

4 Grendel's mother discovers the body of her son and says, 'That horrible Geat (*kill*) .... my son.'

5 Beowulf says to Hrothgar just before he leaves for home, 'You (*be*) .... very generous, but now it is time for me to leave.'

6 Beowulf returned to his king, Hygelac, and said, 'Hrothgar (*be*) .... very kind and generous to me.'

Before you read

1 Reading pictures

Look at the illustration on page 67. Talk about your ideas in pairs or small groups, and then tell the class what you think.

1 Whose head is Beowulf holding?

2 What part of the sword is left? (If you can't remember the word, look back at page 12.)

3 Why do you think only this part of the sword is left?

4 What do you think Beowulf will do with this part of the sword?

5 What other ideas does the illustration suggest?

2 What happens next?

Look at the three questions below. Talk about your ideas in pairs or small groups, and then tell the class what you think.

1 Chapter Six begins like this:
Hrothgar and his men were still by the side of the lake, watching for any sign of Beowulf. Suddenly they saw a huge wave, and the water turned red with blood.

How do you think Hrothgar and his men will react when they see the blood in the water?

A They will think that the fight is over, and that Grendel's mother has killed Beowulf.

B They will think that the fight is over, and that Beowulf has killed Grendel's mother.

C They will think that the fight is still going on, and that Beowulf is winning.

D They will think that the fight is still going on, and that Grendel's mother is winning.

E Your idea: ....

2 This is a sentence from Chapter Six:
Beowulf looked round the monster's court, and he saw a lot of rich treasure there.

What do you think Beowulf will do?

A He will destroy the treasure.

B He will take the treasure, and give it to Hrothgar.

C He will take the treasure, and give it to his followers.

D He will leave all the treasure where it is.

E Your idea: ....

3 If Grendel's mother is dead, what do you think will happen to the snakes in the sea?

A They will become more aggressive; they will attack Beowulf.

B They will disappear completely.

C They will increase in number; they will attack Beowulf.

A They will become friendly; they will help Beowulf swim to the surface.

E Your idea: ....

Now read and/or listen to Chapter Six and find out if your ideas were right.

CHAPTER **SIX**

8

Hrothgar and his men were still by the side of the lake, watching for any sign of Beowulf. Suddenly they saw a huge wave, and the water turned red with blood. Hrothgar's advisers shook [1] their heads sadly. They thought the hero had surely met his death down there in the depths. [2] They did not expect to see Beowulf come back to them.

The king and his men waited for some time longer, and then they went back to Heorot Hall. Beowulf's men, however, remained where they were. They had no hope that Beowulf would survive, but they stayed all the same.

At the bottom of the lake Beowulf watched as the sword he had used to kill Grendel's mother began to melt. [3] It dissolved the same way that the frost [4] dissolves when the sun is warm. Beowulf looked round the monster's court, and he saw a lot of rich treasure there. He took nothing with him when he left, however, except the monster's head and the sword hilt.

He swam upwards through the water. The snakes had gone now that the monster was dead, and the water no longer burned. Beowulf swam strongly for the land, pulling his heavy load behind him.

1. **shook** : (*shake, shook, shaken*) moved from side to side.
2. **in the depths** : (here) at the bottom of the lake.
3. **melt** : turn to liquid.
4. **frost** : very thin layer of ice.

The Geats were full of joy when they saw their hero reach the land. They helped him to take off his armour, and to carry the monster's head. They put the head on a spear, and they set off for Hrothgar's Hall.

Beowulf showed the king the monster's head when he arrived at the Hall. He had won his victory, and spoke to the king:

'We are happy to bring you this sign of our victory. The battle under the water was a difficult one, and I nearly died down there. I could not have done it without God's help. Hrunting is a good sword, but it failed me in the battle. Luckily, I found another sword, an old one, and it was with this that I killed the monster. Now you can sleep safely, I promise you. That terrible monster will not disturb you again.'

Beowulf gave the sword hilt to the king as a present. Hrothgar examined it carefully, and then he spoke:

'A king like me, who has promised to protect truth and to defend tradition, has the right to say that a warrior like Beowulf will achieve [1] great things in his life. You are famous now, Beowulf, everybody knows who you are. And because I am wise, I want to share my wisdom with you.'

Then Hrothgar gave Beowulf this advice:

'It is wonderful how God allows a man to achieve many things and to become powerful in his own land. But then that man forgets that he has to die one day. He lives for pleasure, and thinks nothing of old age and sickness. [2] He does not worry about his enemies. He sees the whole world obey him, and he becomes

1. **achieve** : succeed in doing.
2. **sickness** : illness.

proud. He ceases [1] to look around him. Then, one day, a killer comes after him, someone with a bow. [2] The killer strikes at him, and the proud man is hit in the heart. Now the demon comes to him, and makes everything bitter. Nothing has meaning for him any more, and he ignores old customs. His body dies, and the man's goods are given to someone else who does not take care of them.'

The king looked at Beowulf for a moment, and then he went on:

'Do not fall into that trap, [3] my friend. Put your trust in eternal things. Do not be proud of your strength, which does not last forever. Remember that you can be destroyed by sickness, by the sword, or by old age. Death will come to you one day.'

Everyone was now listening to Hrothgar's words of wisdom. He went on:

'I was like that, you see. I ruled for fifty years. I defended my people with my sword. I thought that I had no more enemies. Then Grendel appeared, and he destroyed the land. I thank God I have seen this monster's head after all my sufferings.'

1. **ceases** : stops.
2. **bow** [bəʊ] : curved weapon made of wood.
3. **do not fall into that trap** : (here) do not make that mistake.

The text and **beyond**

1 Comprehension check

Answer the questions below.

1 Why were Hrothgar's advisers sure that Grendel's mother had killed Beowulf?

2 Name three things that happened because Grendel's mother was dead.

3 What did Beowulf bring back with him from the bottom of the mere?

4 According to Hrothgar, what do powerful men forget?

5 What is Hrothgar's advice to Beowulf?

6 What personal experience made Hrothgar wish to give Beowulf that advice?

2 Speaking

Why do you think Beowulf didn't bring any of the treasure back with him?

3 Writing

Hrothgar, like a good father, wants to tell his sons about the meaning of life. Imagine you are Hrothgar: write a letter of between 120 and 180 words, including the points below:

— Hrothgar's family of kings and his successful reign
— the building of Heorot Hall
— Grendel
— Grendel's mother

My dearest sons

Put your trust in eternal things.

....

....

This is what my long life, full of both happiness and sorrow, has taught me.

Your loving father

4 Swords

Read the article about swords below, and then say which paragraph (1st, 2nd, 3rd or 4th) talks about:

A ☐ What ancient swords looked like
B ☐ The effectiveness of ancient swords as weapons
C ☐ The importance of swords among the early Anglo-Saxons
D ☐ The importance of swords in ancient societies and cultures in general

The sword is a weapon of individual combat, and so, in ancient times, it was associated with great leaders and heroes. Also, in ancient times the materials needed for making swords were not very common, which made them even more the weapon of kings and noble warriors. Ancient legends and myths in many cultures often give magical qualities to swords as well, and even today swords are used in special ceremonies.

Among the early Germanic peoples, too, it was the most prestigious weapon, but not the most common one: spears, which were made of wood and a little bit of iron, were the weapon of the common soldiers. Swords were very valuable and were often handed down from generation to generation, or were received or given as gifts by great warriors and kings. Swords were considered to have a greater value if they had a history or had belonged to a famous warrior. Perhaps this was because people thought that they contained in some way the bravery of their previous owners.

The blades (the parts of the swords used for cutting) were between 72 - 80 cm long and up to 7.5 cm wide. In Anglo-Saxon times, swords usually had hilts made up of layers of organic material such as wood or bone. They were often decorated or even completely covered by bronze, gold and silver. Some were even decorated with precious stones.

It seems possible that Anglo-Saxon swords were capable of cutting through armour, although modern tests do not support this theory entirely. It is possible that the heavy weight of the blade was used to break bones and crush internal organs. A number of skeletons found in ancient graves from northern Europe show just how dangerous a sword could be even when a man was protected by armour. There is evidence of terrible injuries, although in some cases the bone has grown back, meaning that the man continued to live even after such a horrific injury.

5 Comprehension check

Now find examples in *Beowulf* that support what you have read in the article, and make notes in the table below. The first one (0) has been done for you.

0	The special qualities of swords	**A** Ancient legends and myths often give magical qualities to swords. **B** Unferth gave Beowulf a magical sword called Hrunting.
1	The people who used swords in ancient times	
2	The value of swords	
3	How a sword is made	
4	The effectiveness of swords	

6 Heroes and their weapons

Think of heroes (and villains!) from legends, literature and films in your culture and English-speaking and other cultures, both old and modern. Are they associated with special weapons? Did they ever give names to their weapons? In pairs or small groups, make a list of at least three characters and their weapons, and then compare your ideas in class.

Some characters to get you started are: King Arthur, the characters from *The Lord of the Rings*, and so on...

7 Discussion

In many modern fantasy films the characters fight with swords, even though highly developed technological weapons are available to them. Sometimes they do not use weapons at all, only martial arts. Why do you think this is?

Robin Hood, played by Hollywood idol Eroll Flynn (1909-59) in *The Adventures of Robin Hood* (directed by Michael Curtiz, 1939). Robin Hood did not rely only on his bow; he was also good with a sword. (The container for arrows that Robin has here is a called a quiver. Quivers could contain up to 24 arrows.)

8 Lurking horrors

to lurk (regular verb): if someone or something lurks somewhere, they wait secretly and silently. They usually intend to do something bad.

Look at the picture on page 77. People have always been afraid of what might lurk in the sea; this is why there are so many films about sharks and other creatures. And in *Beowulf* monsters also lurk in the dark outside the mead hall. In films and fiction, who – or what – often lurks where?

T: GRADE 7

9 Speaking – early memories

Prepare to have a conversation about your early childhood memories. What were you afraid of? What things made you happy? What other memories do you have?

Before you read

1 Listening

Do not look at pages 75-76. Listen to the first section of Chapter Seven and complete the sentences.

1 The Geats prepared to leave because they wanted to ....
2 Beowulf gave Unferth back his ....
3 If other enemies come to attack Hrothgar, Beowulf .... to help them.
4 If Hrethric visits the Geats he will find many ....
5 According to Hrothgar, if Hygelac dies, Beowulf will be a great ....
6 Beowulf made the Geats and the Danes friends despite ....
7 Hrothgar says that he will be Beowulf's friend ....
8 Hrothgar was sad when Beowulf left because he thought ....

9 **The next day Beowulf and his Geats prepared to leave Denmark.** They were impatient to go back to their own country. Beowulf gave Hrunting back to Unferth, and thanked him for the use of it. He said it had been useful to him, and he did not blame [1] Unferth for its failure in the battle.

The Geats came into the throne room to salute [2] Hrothgar. Beowulf spoke:

'We want to return now to our home. We have been welcomed here, and you have treated us well. If I can do anything more for you, my lord, I shall be ready to do it. If enemies come to your kingdom I will cross the sea once more to help you against them. I know King Hygelac will also be willing to help you if you need us. If your son Hrethric wants to travel and he comes to visit the Geats, he will find many friends there.'

Hrothgar listened to Beowulf's words, and then he replied:

'God sent you those words, my friend. You are strong in body, and you are strong in mind. If anything bad happens to Hygelac, if some enemy should kill him, or some sickness destroy him, you would be an excellent king for the Geats. I like you, Beowulf. You have brought friendship between the Geats and the Danes,

1. **blame** : think he was responsible.
2. **salute** : (here) say goodbye to.

despite [1] the hatreds of the past. I will be the Geats' friend as long as I live.'

Then Hrothgar gave Beowulf more treasures and told him to set out on his journey. The king embraced the hero, and tears were in the old man's eyes. He feared [2] he would never see the hero again, and this thought made him sad.

Beowulf and the Geats marched to the sea. They passed the watchman, who rode up to say goodbye to them. Then they loaded their ship with Hrothgar's gifts and sailed away.

Their journey across the sea was a quick one, and they soon arrived home. The Geat watchman ran to welcome them home, and he moored [3] their boat for them. Then the treasure was carried ashore, and Beowulf and his men went to King Hygelac's stronghold.

Hygelac greeted the hero and his men warmly. Queen Hygd passed the cup to each of them in a kindly way. Then the king began to ask Beowulf about his exploits. He wanted to know everything that had happened. The king put his questions:

'What happened on your journey? Did you help Hrothgar? Your adventure worried me, I was afraid for you. I thank God you have returned here safely.'

Now Beowulf answered the king's anxious questions:

'Everything was done well. Hrothgar welcomed us and asked us to sit with his sons in the Hall. He treated us well.'

Then Beowulf spoke about the enmity [4] between the Danes

1. **despite** : although there were (see page 81).
2. **feared** : was afraid, worried.
3. **moored** : tied to the land.
4. **enmity** : long-lasting hatred.

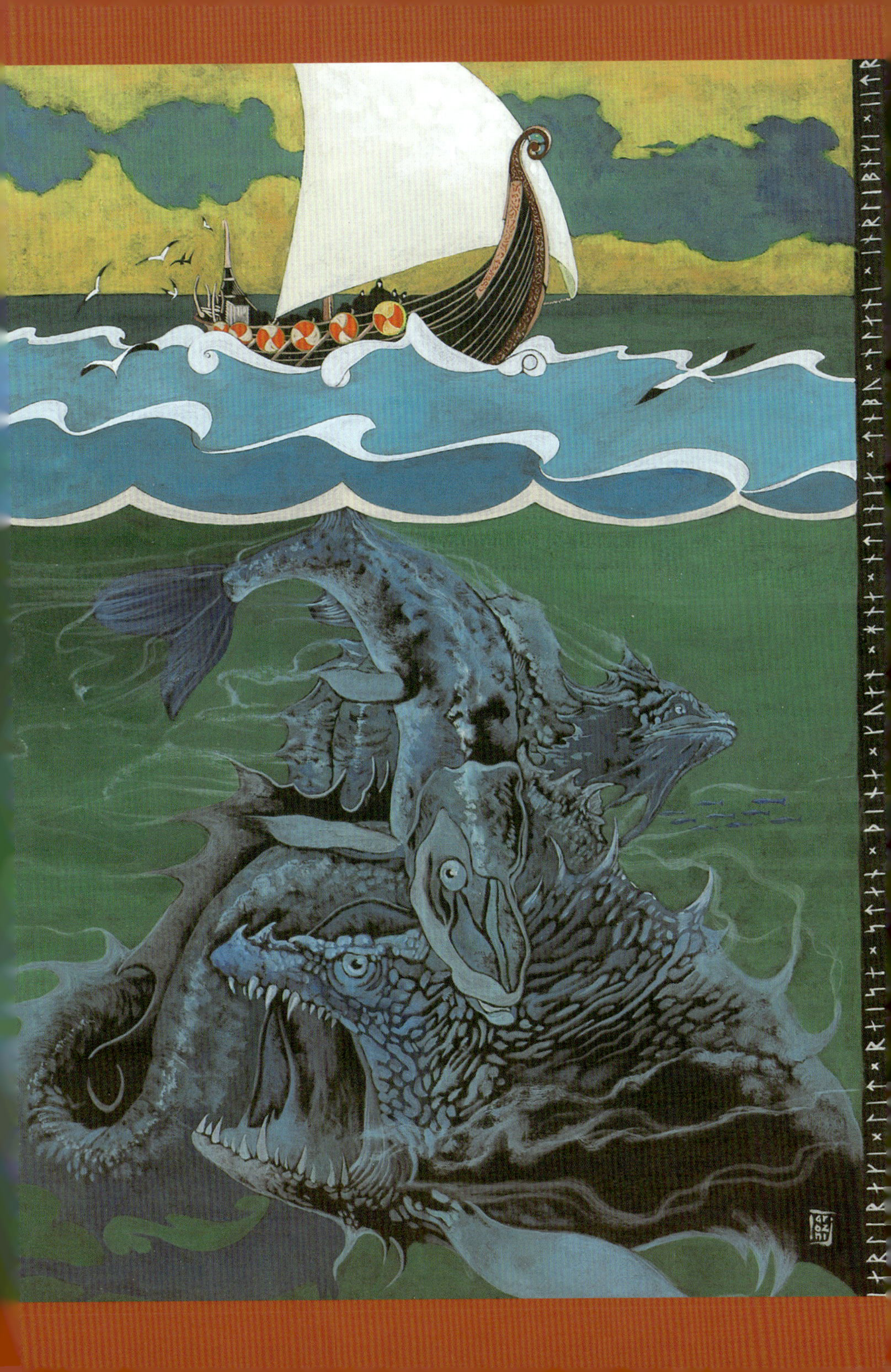

and the Heathobards:

'Hrothgar's daughter, Freawaru, is going to marry Ingeld the Heathobard. They hope the marriage will make peace between the Danes and the Heathobards,[1] but I am not so sure about that. How will the Heathobards feel when the Danes come to the wedding? The Danes will be wearing some of the armour they took from the Heathobard warriors when they defeated them. Some old Heathobard who remembers those days will look at the Danes. He will recognise a piece of armour that used to belong to an old friend who died in the slaughter.[2] Then he will become bitter with his memories. He will say to the dead man's son, "That's your father's sword, young fellow[3] — the one he wore the day he went to fight the Danes". Then the young man will get up and avenge his father's death. The Danes and the Heathobards will rise angrily to their feet. Ingeld will look at his young wife Freawaru and begin to hate her because of the violent past.'

Now Beowulf told King Hygelac about his encounter with Grendel. He described how he had fought the monster in Heorot Hall, and how he had killed him there. Then he described the fight with Grendel's mother, and the successful conclusion to it.

When Beowulf stopped speaking, he called for the gifts that he had received from Hrothgar. He presented these to Hygelac. He gave the king the standard, the helmet and the armour, and the fine horses. He gave Queen Hygd the magnificent torque that Hrothgar's queen had given him. Beowulf kept nothing for himself. He behaved with full honour.

1. **Heathobards** : A Germanic people, neighbours but enemies of the Danes.
2. **slaughter** [slɔːtə] : massacre.
3. **young fellow** : young man.

The text and **beyond**

FCE **1** **Comprehension check**

For the questions below, choose the answer (A, B, C or D) which you think is best according to the text.

1 How did Beowulf say goodbye to Unferth?

A ☐ He thanked him and gave him many treasures and gold.
B ☐ He thanked him for his sword and gave it back to him.
C ☐ He told him that the sword had been of no use to him.
D ☐ He told him that his sword had been important for him.

2 For what reason would Beowulf return to Denmark?

A ☐ if King Hrothgar wanted to give him more gifts
B ☐ if King Hrothgar's son wanted to see Beowulf again
C ☐ if enemies attacked Denmark
D ☐ if Unferth asked him to come back

3 The Danes want Hrothgar's daughter to marry Ingeld because

A ☐ they think that it will be a happy marriage.
B ☐ they think that Ingeld has a lot of treasures.
C ☐ they know that Beowulf will approve of it.
D ☐ they hope the Heathobards will stop hating the Danes.

4 Beowulf thinks there will be a fight at the wedding because

A ☐ the Danes who come to the wedding will wear the armour of the people they killed in battle.
B ☐ the Heathobards will get angry when they see a Dane marry a Heathobard, and this will cause a fight.
C ☐ the Heathobards will see the Danes wearing armour and think that they want to fight.
D ☐ the Danes will accuse the Heathobards of stealing their armour.

5 Beowulf thinks Ingeld will begin to hate Freawaru because

A ☐ her family fought with his family in the past.
B ☐ she has Ingeld's father's sword.
C ☐ she prefers Unferth.
D ☐ she is Hrothgar's daughter.

6 What did Beowulf do with the gifts he received in Denmark?

A ☐ He gave them all to his men.
B ☐ He gave them all to his king and queen.
C ☐ He gave them to the old Heathobards.
D ☐ He kept them for himself.

2 Anglo-Saxon values

What qualities of Anglo-Saxon behaviour can you see in Chapter Seven? Include behaviour that you think is both good and bad by the standards of your culture today.

FCE 3 Sentence transformation

In the questions below, complete the second sentence so that it has a similar meaning to the first sentence, using the word given. Do not change the word given. You must use between two and five words, including the word given. There is an example at the beginning (0).

0 He feared he would never see Beowulf again, and this made him sad.
because
He *was sad because he feared* he would never see the hero again.

1 Hrothgar listened to Beowulf's words, and then he replied.
listening
After .... , Hrothgar replied.

2 God sent you those words.
by
Those words .... God.

3 He said that he did not blame Unferth for its failure in the battle.
you
Beowulf said, 'I .... for its failure in the battle.'

4 Beowulf said, 'He treated us well.'
them
Beowulf said that Hrothgar .... well.

5 They hope the marriage will make peace between the enemies.
marry
They hope that if .... there will be peace between the enemies.

6 'That's your father's sword, young fellow — the one he wore when he went to fight.'
which
'Young fellow, that's the sword .... when he went to fight.'

'You have brought friendship between the Geats and the Danes, despite the hatreds of the past'

Clauses of contrast: **despite** and **although**

Look at these sentences. They all have basically the same meaning.

– ***The Geats and the Danes hated each other in the past****, but you have brought friendship between them.*
– ***Although the Geats and the Danes hated each other in the past****, you have brought friendship between them.*
– ***You have brought friendship between the Geats and the Danes****, despite the hatreds of the past.*

Despite (or **in spite of**) is followed by a noun or pronoun (*this, that, what* or a verb with *-ing*).
Although is followed by a subject and a verb.

Despite *being very hungry, I couldn't eat.*
Despite *my hunger, I couldn't eat.*
Although *I was very hungry, I couldn't eat.*

Although *I hate them, I will make peace with them.*
Despite *my hatred for them, I will make peace with them.* Or
Despite *my hating them, I will make peace with them.*

Although is more common in spoken English. You find **despite** and **in spite of** more in written English than in spoken English. You can see this when you compare the different styles of the following:

– ***Although*** *the film was really long, I was never bored.* (spoken)
– ***Despite*** *its length, the film was not boring.* (written)

4 Contrast: *despite* and *although*

Rewrite the following sentences using either *despite* or *although*. There is an example at the beginning (0).

0 Although Grendel was incredibly strong, Beowulf pulled off his arm. (*despite*)
strength
Despite Grendel's incredible strength, Beowulf pulled off his arm.

1 Despite the antiquity of *Beowulf*, it is still an exciting story. (*although*)
old
....

2 Although Unferth's sword failed during the battle, Beowulf thanked him for it. (*despite*)
failure
....

3 Although I want to go home, I will stay here and fight the monster. (*despite*)
homesickness
....

4 You must die in the end despite your greatness. (*although*)
great
....

5 Despite their past love, they now hate each other. (*although*)
loved
....

5 Writing and speaking

Write down three or four sentences about friends, members of your family or people that you know. Then compare them in small groups. Do you have the same ideas?

Examples:

Although my dad is quiet, he has a good sense of humour.
I really like going out with my friend Angela, despite the fact that she never arrives on time!

What *Makes an Epic*

In literature, an epic is a long poem on a great subject; the main character is a hero on whose actions the future of an entire people may depend. Epics, therefore, are often of national importance.

There are two kinds. 'Primary' or 'folk' epics were composed in the oral tradition, and often bring together several myths, legends, folk tales and elements of history. They were only written down hundreds of years after they were composed: *Beowulf* is this kind of epic. The oldest is *Gilgamesh* (about 3000 BCE [1]) from Sumer (in modern-day Iraq); the Greek epics the *Iliad* and the *Odyssey* (about 1000 BCE) by the legendary poet Homer are very well-known.

'Secondary' or 'literary' epics are from later historical periods. Their poets wrote them down as they composed them. An early example is Virgil's Latin poem the *Aeneid* (about 30-19 CE). It is about how Aeneas escaped from Troy and, after many dangerous adventures, founded [2] Lavinium, the parent town of Rome.

Homer, from a 2nd century BCE bust. According to tradition, he was blind.

1. **BCE** : abbreviation of *Before the Common Era*, an alternative for BC (*Before Christ*), a way of showing the number of years before the birth of Christ. CE (*Common Era*) is an alternative for AD (*Anno Domini*), for showing the number of years after Christ's birth. Both systems count the years in the same way.
2. **founded** : (*found, founded, founded*) built for the first time.

Both primary and secondary epics have these elements:

1 **the hero:** he has great or even superhuman qualities; the future of a nation – or even the world – may depend on him
2 **the setting:** very wide – things happen in many different places and over a long period
3 **the action:** there are courageous and even superhuman deeds in battle; long, dangerous journeys are common
4 **the supernatural:** gods or supernatural creatures take part, or are often mentioned
5 **the style:** a very 'poetic' style, very different from everyday language; there is often repetition, elaborate greetings and long speeches.

1 Comprehension check

What is the difference between a primary epic and a secondary epic?

2 Contemporary epics

Nowadays, the word 'epic' is used more often about novels and films. In class, think of five well-known books or films that people call 'epics'. In small groups, analyse them according to the five elements of epics listed above. Which of the five most deserves to be called a real 'epic'?

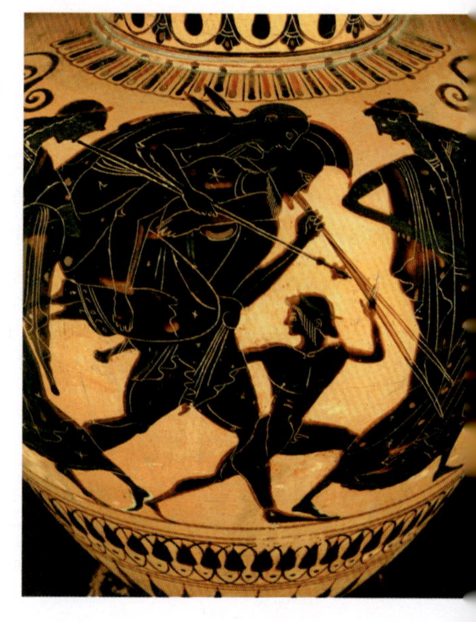

Aeneas carries his father, Anchises, away from Troy. His son, Ascanius, runs in front. **Greek vase painting** (6th century BCE).

3 World epics

A In the table below there are seven epics, both primary and secondary. The dates are all CE. Can you fill in the 4th column with the countries?

Austria/Germany Portugal Spain France England Turkey Italy

Name	Author	Date	Country
La Chanson de Roland	Turold (probably)	about 1100	
Cantar de mío Cid	unknown	1150-1200	
Nibelungenlied	unknown	about 1200	
Dede Korkut	unknown	9th-10th century	
Os Lusiadas	Luís de Camoëns	1572	
Gerusalemme Liberata	Torquato Tasso	1575	
Paradise Lost	John Milton	1667	

B Work in groups. Each group finds out about one of the epics and writes a sentence (maximum 30 words) to say what it is about. (The sentence about the *Aeneid* in the text above is an example.)

C Complete the last line of the table with another epic (perhaps your own national epic) and write a sentence to say what it is about.

Christian Elements in *Beowulf*

The values in *Beowulf* are mostly pagan, but there are some Christian elements, too. Why? When the poem was being composed, the Anglo-Saxons were converting to Christianity, so perhaps for this reason the poem has both pagan and Christian elements. Another explanation is that *Beowulf* is really a pagan poem: the monks [1] who kept the manuscript added the Christian elements. Grendel's relationship to Cain (page 15) seems like a Christian addition.

The contrast between pagan gods and the Christian god is seen early in the story: Hrothgar's advisers *'sometimes ... prayed to false gods for help ... They forgot the real God ...'* (page 18).

There is also a contrast between heroic values and Christianity. After Aeschere's death, for example, Beowulf says to Hrothgar, *'Do not be sad, sir. It is better to avenge a friend's death than to cry over it'* (page 57, top). This desire for revenge comes from the heroic values of a pagan, not Christian, society.

Belief in fate – usually a pagan idea about accepting the inevitable [2] – and Christian

Saint Mary's, an **Anglo-Saxon church** in Hampshire, southeast England. Beginning of 11th century.

1. **monks** : members of a religious community who live together.
2. **inevitable** : something that you cannot avoid or fight against.

faith are sometimes seen together. In Chapter Eight Beowulf feels that a dragon is sent by God to punish him – so, caused by his actions not by fate – but he has pagan desire for revenge: *'Beowulf … thought he had offended God ... He decided to take his revenge against the dragon.'* (page 90). But before the fight he feels that it is his fate to die: *'… he felt that his death was near.'* (page 91, top)

Some critics think that the atmosphere of sadness in the poem is because the poet knew the old pagan, heroic way of life was disappearing, to be replaced by a new, Christian society.

1 Comprehension check

A Give two explanations of why there are Christian elements in *Beowulf*.

B Give an example of a Christian element in *Beowulf*.

C Give an example of a heroic element in *Beowulf*.

2 Discussion

In what you have read so far of *Beowulf*, does it feel more pagan, more Christian, or a mixture of both? And, do *you* think that the atmosphere is sad? Refer to the story to support your views.

Before you read

1 Reading pictures

Turn over the page and look at the picture on page 89 for five seconds – no more! Then, in groups, compare everything you can remember.

How do you think what you have seen will come into the story? Make a prediction, then read and/or listen to Chapter Eight and find out.

10

Beowulf's reputation among the Geats was great now. King Hygelac had not thought highly of the young hero before, but all that changed after he heard about Beowulf's adventures. The king rewarded him generously for his courage, giving him a sword and land.

The years passed, and the Geats became involved in wars with their enemies. Hygelac was killed in battle, and Beowulf became king. He ruled well for fifty years, and grew into old age with wisdom.

Now a new danger threatened the Geat kingdom. There was an underground barrow,[1] which contained a great quantity of treasure. The treasure had belonged to a noble family a long time before, but the family had been destroyed in war. A lone[2] survivor of their blood[3] had buried their riches in the ground.

Three centuries earlier a dragon had found the place and made its home there. He guarded the treasure in peace and quiet. No one came to disturb the dragon's rest[4] beneath the ground.

Now a foolish[5] man went into the dragon's hiding-place and

1. **barrow** : place where Anglo-Saxons buried the dead.
2. **a lone** : the only.
3. **blood** : (here) family.
4. **rest** : (here) sleep.
5. **foolish** : stupid.

stole a jewelled goblet.[1] The thief took the goblet back to his master, and told him where the treasure could be found.

The dragon awoke from his sleep and was furious at his loss.

1. **jewelled goblet** : magnificent cup decorated with jewels.

He saw the tracks of human feet, and emerged from the barrow when it was dark. He breathed fire in his anger, and wanted his revenge. He attacked the people on the land, burning their homes and killing everyone he found.

The Geat nation was afraid of the terrible destruction that the dragon brought with him. They feared his attacks in the darkness, the flames and death he carried with him.

One day Beowulf heard bad news. The dragon had come to his own house and burnt the throne room.

Beowulf was troubled [1] at the news. He thought he had offended God in some way. He decided to take his revenge against the dragon. He was too proud to use his whole army in the battle, and he was not afraid of the dragon's strength. He thought he was stronger than the beast. [2]

He remembered all his past adventures, and this gave him courage. He remembered his battles against Grendel and the monster's mother. He remembered how he had helped the Geats after their king Hygelac was killed. He had defeated the Geats' enemies with his sword, and had protected Hygelac's son Heardred. He had become king after Heardred's death. Later he had avenged that death. When he thought of all these things, he was not afraid.

Beowulf took eleven warriors with him, and went out to look for the dragon. By now he understood what had happened. He had found the thief who had taken the goblet, and he made that man come with him. He told the thief to show him where the

1. **troubled** : worried.
2. **beast** : wild animal (here, the dragon).

dragon's barrow was. The thief led them to the coast, and showed them the place.

Beowulf sat at the top of the cliffs. He was sad because he felt that his death was near. He wished the Geats who had served with him good fortune [1] in the future. Now he spoke to them:

'I have survived many dangers in my life. I came to the court when I was young, and I saw trouble among the king's family and war against our enemies. Hygelac gave me land to reward me for my loyalty to him. I always took my place at the front of the battle — and I shall fight like that until the end.'

Beowulf made a final promise to his men:

'I was often in danger when I was young. Now that I am old, I will risk it once again for the sake of glory. [2] I will fight that dragon if he comes out of the barrow.'

Then the warrior hero said goodbye to his friends. He ordered them to remain where they were so that they could see the outcome [3] of the fight.

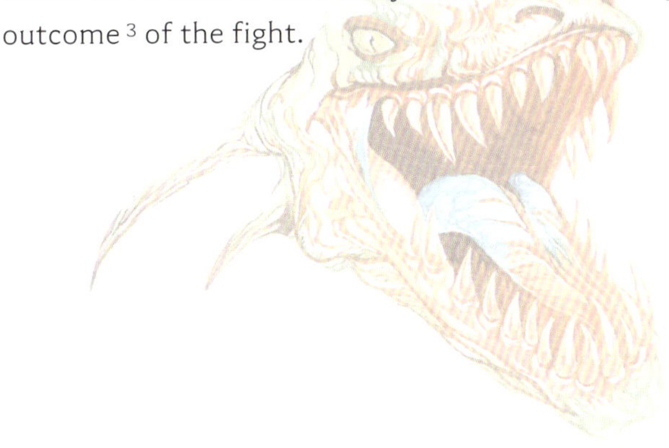

1. **fortune** : luck.
2. **for the sake of glory** : in the name of honour.
3. **outcome** : result.

The text and **beyond**

1 Comprehension check

Say whether the following statements are True (T) or False (F). Correct the false ones.

		T	F
1	Beowulf became king after King Hrothgar died.	☐	☐
2	Beowulf ruled the Geats for fifty years.	☐	☐
3	The dragon guarded a treasure that once belonged to a noble family.	☐	☐
4	The dragon had destroyed the noble family.	☐	☐
5	The dragon woke up because Beowulf stole some of the treasure from the barrow.	☐	☐
6	When Beowulf first heard about the dragon he blamed himself for its arrival.	☐	☐
7	Beowulf later discovered that a thief had disturbed the dragon's rest.	☐	☐
8	Beowulf was sad before the battle with the dragon because he felt that he was soon going to die.	☐	☐

2 Anglo-Saxon values

What qualities of Anglo-Saxon heroic behaviour can you see in Chapter Eight?

3 Dragons!

Dragons are not only found in old epics: they are as popular today as ever. If you do a search for just the word 'dragon' on the Internet you will get millions of hits! In pairs, use encyclopaedias or refined searches on the Internet to find out some more information on some of the topics listed on the next page. Choose the topics that interest you most.

- The nature and appearance of dragons in general: legendary giant lizards, often with wings and poisonous or fiery breath
- In ancient times dragons were often symbols of destruction and evil
- For ancient Hebrews they are symbols of death and evil. This continues in apocalyptic Christian writings, for example the *Book of Revelation*, the last book of the Bible
- For ancient Greeks and Romans dragons were protective and fierce; dragons also communicate the secrets of the Earth to humans
- Dragons were used on Roman battle standards
- The legend of Saint George and the dragon
- In the Taoist religion of China dragons are gods, and for the Chinese dragons are symbols of good luck
- Dragons in art
- Dragons in film

T: GRADE 7

4 Speaking

Prepare a presentation on the topic of dragons for the rest of the class (maximum 5 minutes). Use illustrations, diagrams or other suitable material to illustrate your topic. Be prepared to answer questions from the rest of the class.

5 Vocabulary

Here is your final battle with the words from Chapters 1-8:

Across

1 past of *swing*
2 where the dragon's treasure was hidden
3 fighter
4 When the dragon burnt the throne room, Beowulf thought he had offended ...
5 past of *flee* (page 36)
6 dead body
7 marks (page 57)
8 hurt with a knife
9 magnificent drinking cup
10 celebration with eating and drinking
11 stop (page 69)

Down

1 an illegal killing
2 covered with blood (page 15)
3 past of *spring*
4 what Beowulf used to kill Grendel's mother
5 brought together (page 14)
6 destiny
7 brutal killing (page 78)
8 make happier (page 57)
9 wild animal

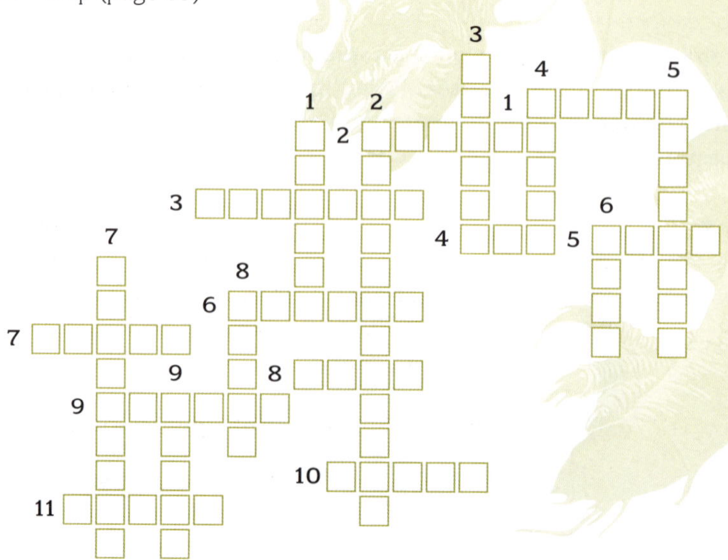

Before you read

1 Fill in the gaps

Do not look at pages 96-97. Use the words in the box to fill in the gaps.

fight danger backwards stop destiny save flames ready shield towards voice gave continued barrow loyal

Beowulf saw a stone arch at the entrance to the barrow. A stream of hot water flowed out of the entrance. It would be difficult for him to (**1**) .... the dragon inside there. He went (**2**) .... the entrance and shouted a challenge to the beast. His voice echoed loudly in the (**3**) ....
The dragon heard the human (**4**) .... and was enraged. He emerged from the barrow, breathing fire as he came. He was (**5**) .... for battle.
Beowulf stood ready for the beast with his sword and (**6**) ....
The dragon turned around him, but the warrior hero did not flinch. Soon the dragon's (**7**) .... covered the place where he stood. His shield did not protect him from the heat and smoke. He raised his sword and (**8**) .... a mighty blow at the furious beast, but his sword did not (**9**) .... the dragon.
The dragon (**10**) .... to send out flames. Beowulf's sword had failed him, and he had to step (**11**) .... It was not easy for him to retreat from an enemy. It was Beowulf's (**12**) .... that day to leave this life.
Now the dragon attacked again. Beowulf was in (**13**) ...., and there was no help from his friends. All of them wanted to run away to (**14**) .... their lives. Only Wiglaf remained with the king. He called to his companions to stay and fight the dragon with him:
'We all promised to be (**15**) .... to our king, and he presented us with valuable gifts and weapons.'

11 **Now read or listen to Chapter Nine to find out if you were right.**

Beowulf saw a stone arch [1] at the entrance to the barrow. A stream of hot water flowed out of the entrance. It would be difficult for him to fight the dragon inside there. He went towards the entrance and shouted a challenge [2] to the beast. His voice echoed loudly in the barrow.

The dragon heard the human voice and was enraged. [3] He emerged from the barrow, breathing fire as he came. He was ready for battle.

Beowulf stood ready for the beast with his sword and shield. The dragon turned around him, but the warrior hero did not flinch. [4] Soon the dragon's flames covered the place where he stood. His shield did not protect him from the heat and smoke. He raised his sword and gave a mighty blow [5] at the furious beast, but his sword did not stop the dragon.

The dragon continued to send out flames. Beowulf's sword had failed him, and he had to step backwards. It was not easy for him to retreat [6] from an enemy. It was Beowulf's destiny that day to leave this life.

1. **arch** :
2. **challenge** : invitation to fight.
3. **enraged** : very angry.
4. **flinch** : move away in fear.
5. **gave a mighty blow** : hit hard.
6. **retreat** : go backwards.

Now the dragon attacked again. Beowulf was in danger, and there was no help from his friends. All of them wanted to run away to save their lives. Only Wiglaf remained with the king. He called to his companions to stay and fight the dragon with him:

'We all promised to be loyal to our king, and he presented us with valuable gifts and weapons. Now he needs our help. Let's go to him and bring him safe out of the dragon's flame and fire.'

It was no use. Wiglaf's companions fled in fear. He drew his sword and moved forwards to Beowulf's side. He was a young man, and this was his first battle. He encouraged Beowulf with his words to him:

'Go on, my lord. Do everything you promised that you would. Your courage has made you a famous man. Defend yourself, and I will stand beside you.'

The dragon came forward once again, and Wiglaf's shield did not protect him from the heat. Beowulf covered him with his own shield. Then the warrior hero gathered his strength together and delivered a great blow with his sword. This time the sword broke over the dragon's head.

The dragon was eager [1] for blood now. He breathed fire over Beowulf and ran in quickly. Then he bit deeply into the warrior's neck. Blood flowed from the wound. Beowulf was dying.

Wiglaf saw that the king's life was in danger. He stepped forward and plunged [2] his sword into the beast's belly. [3] Now the dragon bled, and his flames grew weaker.

Beowulf made a final effort. [4] He drew out a knife from his

1. **eager** : (here) hungry.
2. **plunged** : pushed in with force.
3. **belly** : stomach.
4. **made a final effort** : used the last of his energy.

belt. He stabbed the dragon in the side, killing his enemy. Wiglaf and Beowulf had destroyed the dragon.

Beowulf's wound began to hurt, and he realised that the dragon had poisoned him. He felt sick and weak, and he went to sit down. Wiglaf washed his wounds, and did everything he could to make Beowulf comfortable. Beowulf knew that he was dying, and he spoke to Wiglaf:

'I have ruled for fifty years. No enemy could frighten me. I always did the best I could, and was kind to my people. This knowledge comforts me now that I am dying. I have done nothing to make God angry with me.'

Then Beowulf gave Wiglaf his orders:

'Go and take out the treasure from the barrow. I want to see it before I die.'

Wiglaf hurried to obey the king. He went into the barrow, and there he saw the dragon's magnificent treasure. He picked up the treasure quickly and rushed back to Beowulf. He hoped that he would find the king alive when he returned to him. Beowulf opened his eyes and looked at the treasure. Then he spoke:

'I thank God that I have seen this treasure. Now I can leave it to my people when I die. You, Wiglaf, must look after them when I am gone. Order my soldiers to build a barrow on the cliffs near the coast. I want it high up on the cliffs, so that sailors will see it as they cross the sea. They will call it Beowulf's barrow.'

Then the king took off the golden collar that he wore. He gave it to the young man with these words:

'You are the last of us.'

The text and **beyond**

1 Comprehension check

Answer the questions below.

1 Why did Beowulf shout a challenge to the dragon at the entrance of the barrow?

2 Why did Beowulf have to retreat from the dragon at the start of their battle?

3 Where did the dragon fight Beowulf?

4 Who killed the dragon?

5 How did the dragon kill Beowulf?

6 Why is Beowulf at peace before he dies?

7 What does Beowulf say to do with the treasure?

8 Why does Beowulf want to have his barrow on a cliff near the coast?

2 Use your answers from above to describe how Beowulf acted heroically in his last adventure.

3 Listening

Listen to the interview about the discovery of the great Anglo-Saxon treasure of Sutton Hoo, and complete the sentences. (You will explore these treasures in the Internet project on page 112.)

1 Dr Jean Smith has written many ....

2 Sutton Hoo is a hill on the Suffolk ....

3 Spiritualism is the belief that you can ....

4 Mrs Pretty had a dream about ....

5 A dowser is a person who uses a forked stick to.............................. .

6 Mr Basil Brown arrived at Sutton Hoo ....

7 The archaeologist Basil Brown began digging in ....

8 Lots of .... were found in the first funeral mounds.

9 However the great discovery was made in ....

10 King Raewald ruled in that area from .... to ....

'I have ruled for fifty years'

The Present Perfect (4)

Look at this sentence:

*I **have ruled** for fifty years* → *I began to rule fifty years ago and I still rule today.*

If we wish to talk about an action that began in the past and continues in the present* we use the Present Perfect.
We prefer to use the Present Perfect Simple for longer time periods or permanent situations:

*I **have worked** here since 1982.*
*I **have lived** here for thirty years.*

Note that the preposition *since* is used for a point in time (e.g. 2001); *for* is used for a period (e.g. ten years).

But for shorter time periods or temporary situations, we prefer to use the Present Perfect Continuous:

*I **have been working** here for two weeks.*
*I **have been living** in Paris for six months.*

The questions in both cases begin with '**how long**?':

***How long** have you lived here?*
***How long** have you been studying English?*

* Remember that if the action began and ended in the past we use the Past Simple:
*I **lived** in Rome for eight years, but now I live in Florence.*

Note that some verbs are not used in the continuous tenses, so we cannot use them with the Present Perfect Continuous: *be, love, hate, know, have* (when it means 'possess').

4 Past or perfect?

Put the verbs in the Past Simple, Present Perfect Simple or Present Perfect Continuous according to the context.

Example:

JOHN: Do you know Harriet?

PETER: Yes, I do. I (*know*) ...have known... her since I was a little boy.

1 I (*wait*) .... for the bus for more than an hour, and then I decided to take a taxi.

2 I (*wait*) .... for the bus for more than an hour. I think I'll take taxi.

3 How long (*you/have*) .... that car?

4 TIM: How long (*you/sit*) .... in the departure lounge?
LOUIS: We (*sit*) .... there for two hours before they finally let us board the plane.

5 Darling, I (*love*) .... you since I first saw you!

6 You (*study*) .... hard since this morning. Stop and take a break. You look exhausted.

7 ROB: Can you speak Spanish?
EMMA: Yes, I (*study*) .... it for three years when I was a university student.

8 SAMANTHA: How long (*you/be married*) ....?
KATIE: We (*be married*) .... forty years. In fact, we have just celebrated our wedding anniversary.

Before you read

13 FCE

1 Listening

Listen to Chapter Ten and say whether the following sentences are true (T) or false (F). Then read the text and correct the false ones.

		T	F
1	Wiglaf was happy to see his companions on return.	☐	☐
2	According to Wiglaf, the Geats' enemies will attack when they hear about the cowardice of Beowulf's companions and about Beowulf's death.	☐	☐
3	The warriors burned the dragon's body.	☐	☐
4	At Beowulf's funeral a woman sang of the Geats' great future.	☐	☐
5	They built the barrow in ten days.	☐	☐
6	They buried the dragon's treasure next to Beowulf.	☐	☐

CHAPTER TEN

13

1 **Beowulf's companions who had run away from the dragon now came back.** They were ashamed, and they stood watching as Wiglaf tried to revive [1] their king. Wiglaf looked up at them and spoke these words angrily:

'Beowulf gave you weapons and other gifts, but it was useless. When he needed you, you deserted [2] him. Yet God allowed him to kill the dragon. I could not do much for him during the battle, but I tried to help him. I managed to wound the beast myself, but there were not enough of us.'

Wiglaf now spoke of his fears for the future:

2 'When our enemies hear about your cowardice [3] today, they will come to destroy our nation. The Franks [4] and the Frisians will soon know that our king is dead. They will soon come here with their warriors. The Swedes will come as well. When Beowulf was king he protected us and kept us safe. He looked after the people, but he was also a hero.'

3 Then Wiglaf told the warriors what they had to do. He said

1. **revive** : bring back to life.
2. **deserted** : left him alone.
3. **cowardice** : not having courage.
4. **Franks** : a Germanic people living in modern-day Belgium and France.

that Beowulf's funeral pyre [1] should be a rich one. They should put the treasure he had won from the dragon onto it.

The warriors wept now as they looked down at the body of their king. Next to Beowulf they saw the body of the dragon. Nearby they saw the rich treasure from the barrow. After a few moments Wiglaf spoke again:

4 'It is often dangerous for a man to do as he wants. This is what happened here. Beowulf disturbed the dragon who was guarding this treasure. Our warrior hero found the treasure, but the cost was high. He died as a result of his search. He told me what to do before he died. He said that we should build a barrow for him on the cliffs.'

5 Wiglaf took the warriors into the dragon's hiding-place. They took out the treasure that was still there. Then they threw the dragon's body over the cliff into the sea.

Wiglaf now told them to prepare wood for Beowulf's funeral pyre. The Geat people built a great fire. They put shields and helmets on the fire, as Wiglaf had instructed them to do. Then they placed Beowulf's body on top.

They lit [2] the funeral pyre, and flames and smoke rose into the sky. The noise of the fire was greater than the sound the people made as they wept for their king.

A Geat woman began to sing about her pain and loss. She sang about her fears and her grief [3] for the nation. She sang about the danger of invasion, the threat of enemies. She sang about the death of the Geats, their slavery and humiliation.

1. **funeral pyre** [paɪə] : ceremonial fire on which a dead body is put.
2. **lit** : (*light, lit, lit*) set fire to.
3. **grief** : sadness.

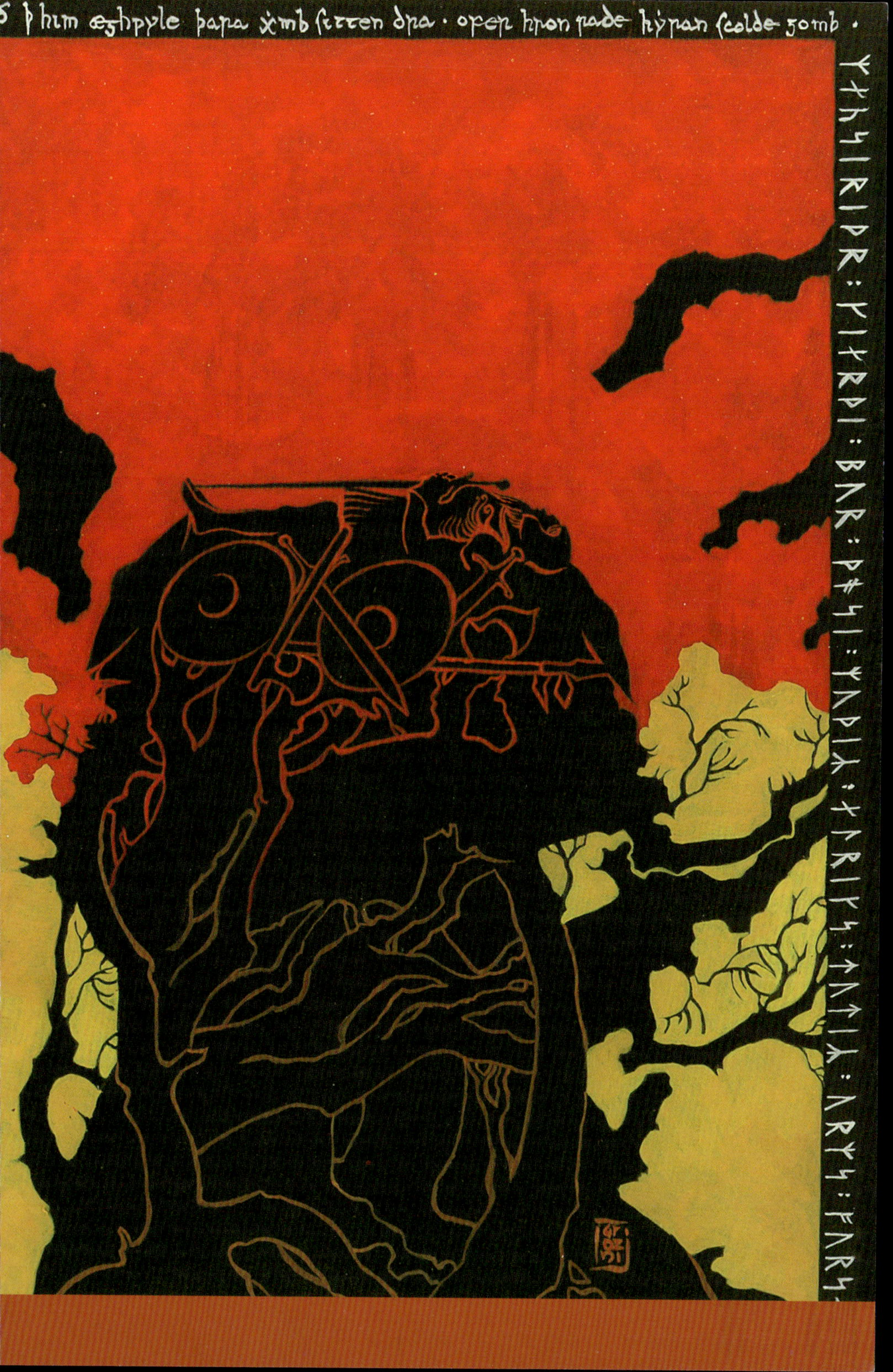
ð þ him æghƿylc þara ymb sittendra · ofer hronrade hyran scolde gomb ·

6 Then the Geats built a large barrow on the cliff. It was big enough for sailors to see from a long way away. It took ten days to finish the work. They took the dust [1] that had been Beowulf, and they placed it inside the barrow. They buried the dragon's treasure next to their dead king.

7 Finally, twelve men rode around the tomb. They were all kings' sons and brave warriors. They sang a dirge [2] for Beowulf, lamenting him [3] as both a man and a king. They sang about his famous deeds, and they thanked God for his greatness. This was how the Geat people mourned [4] their lord. They said that he had been the best king in the whole world, and that he had been very good to his people.

1. **dust** : the remains of Beowulf after being burnt.
2. **dirge** [dɜːdʒ]: sad song, used when a person has died.
3. **lamenting him** : showing their sadness for his death.
4. **mourned** : showed sadness for his death (like *lament*).

The text and **beyond**

1 Comprehension check

Chapter Ten has been divided into seven parts. Choose the best title from the list A-H for each part (1-7). There is one extra title which you do not need to use.

- **A** ☐ Cowardice kills the king
- **B** ☐ Our great day is coming
- **C** ☐ A dragon's jewels to celebrate a great king
- **D** ☐ Do it at your own risk
- **E** ☐ A great tomb for a great man
- **F** ☐ Noblemen sing his greatness
- **G** ☐ Flames of sadness
- **H** ☐ Dark future

2 Speaking

Most readers find a strong feeling of sadness and pessimism at the end of *Beowulf*. Do you feel this? Why, or why not?

3 Writing

You have read about many of the ideal qualities of the Anglo-Saxons:

- Absolute loyalty to your chief and tribe
- Putting your trust in eternal things
- Revenge is better than crying
- Courage and skill in battle
- A sense of honour and the desire for fame

Do you find these qualities admirable? Do you think Beowulf is a good role model for today? Or do you think we need other kinds of heroes? Write a short article (about 200 words) entitled: *Beowulf – a Hero for Today?*

FCE 1 Comprehension check

For the questions below, choose the answer (A, B, C or D) which you think is best according to the text.
Try to answer from memory, without looking back at the text.

1 Why did Hrothgar build a mead hall?
- **A** ☐ He wanted a place to protect him from Grendel.
- **B** ☐ He wanted a place to leave to his sons.
- **C** ☐ He wanted a place to protect him from Grendel's mother.
- **D** ☐ He wanted a place which would be a sign of his power.

2 Who was Grendel?
- **A** ☐ a demon
- **B** ☐ the brother of Abel
- **C** ☐ the brother of Cain
- **D** ☐ a Geat who hated the Danes

3 Who was Beowulf?
- **A** ☐ a Geat lord
- **B** ☐ the king of Geatland
- **C** ☐ the poet of the Danes
- **D** ☐ Hrothgar's brother

4 How did Beowulf want to fight Grendel?
- **A** ☐ with Hrothgar and his warriors
- **B** ☐ with other Geat warriors
- **C** ☐ alone and without any weapons
- **D** ☐ with only his magic sword

5 How did Beowulf kill Grendel?
- **A** ☐ He pulled his arm and shoulder off.
- **B** ☐ He cut his head off.
- **C** ☐ He drowned him.
- **D** ☐ He stabbed him in the heart with his magic sword.

6 Who did King Hrothgar thank for the death of Grendel?
- **A** ☐ God
- **B** ☐ Beowulf
- **C** ☐ the Danes
- **D** ☐ the Geats

7 What did Grendel look like?
- A ☐ a giant lizard
- B ☐ a woman
- C ☐ a man
- D ☐ a man with a snake's head

8 How did Beowulf kill Grendel's mother?
- A ☐ with one of her swords
- B ☐ with her own knife
- C ☐ with his sword
- D ☐ with Hrunting, the sword that Unferth had given him

9 What did Beowulf bring back to King Hrothgar after he had killed Grendel's mother?
- A ☐ all her treasure and her head, which he had cut off
- B ☐ all her weapons and her head, which he had cut off
- C ☐ her head, which he had cut off
- D ☐ the hilt of her sword and her head, which he had cut off

10 Who became the king of the Geats when Hygelac was killed in battle?
- A ☐ Hrothgar
- B ☐ Beowulf
- C ☐ Unferth
- D ☐ Ingeld

11 Why did the dragon begin to attack the Geats?
- A ☐ because it wanted to avenge the death of Grendel and his mother
- B ☐ because it felt that Beowulf was old and could not defend his people
- C ☐ because a thief had stolen a goblet it was guarding
- D ☐ because it wanted to destroy the Geats

12 Why did Wiglaf say that the Franks, Frisians and Swedes would soon attack the Geats after Beowulf's death?
- A ☐ because they had been afraid of Beowulf and now that he was dead they could attack
- B ☐ because they would hear about the treasure and would come to get it
- C ☐ because they knew that Wiglaf was a weak man
- D ☐ because they would hear that all of Beowulf's men, except, Wiglaf, were afraid

2 The Anglo-Saxon view of life

Below is a description of how the pagan Anglo-Saxons saw life. Read it and then answer the questions which follow.

This is how the present life of man on earth, my King, appears to me in comparison with the time after we die, which we know nothing about. You are feasting with your noble warriors in the winter time; the fire is burning in the middle of the mead hall and all inside is warm, while outside there are wintry storms of rain and snow; a little bird flies quickly through the hall. It enters at one door and quickly flies out through the other. For the few moments it is inside the winter storm cannot touch it, but after the briefest moment of peace and warmth inside the mead hall away from the wintry storm, it is outside again in the cold and wind. The life of man appears only for a moment; what follows or what went before, we know nothing about.

1 Does *Beowulf* support this view of life? Why or why not?

2 The passage above comes from the writings of Bede (c. 673-735), an English priest and historian from Anglo-Saxon times: the speaker in the passage is the adviser of an Anglo-Saxon king. What view of life does the story communicate? The story was told to explain why Christianity might be better than the pagan beliefs about death: how does it show this?

3 What does this passage tell us about the importance of the mead hall in Anglo-Saxon culture? Is the same importance given to the mead hall in *Beowulf*?

3 Characters

Which characters might have made the statements below?

Example:

I grew up without my parents. Despite this disadvantage I grew up to be a great warrior and won many battles. Then I even became a great king.
Answer: Shield Sheafson

A I was a great king and ruled well for many years. My victories were many and minstrels sang about them the world over. But my own greatness had to end, and what is even sadder for me as I walk among the dead is to think that my end signalled the end of my own people.

B Once I was a king's favourite and I won many battles with my magic sword, but then another hero came and jealousy consumed me. I told my followers that this hero from a foreign land was just vain and that he had actually lost many challenges. Unfortunately for me, or fortunately for me, this hero killed our worst enemy.

C Loyalty above all! Be loyal to your king and your king will be loyal to you. That is the Anglo-Saxon way. I followed this rule but my companions didn't. I will be honoured forever in the songs of the minstrels and they will be criticised. But my satisfaction is little since my king died and I could not save him.

D Never trust what my enemies say about me. I was doing my job and I never hurt anyone. Then one day a common thief came and stole a goblet, part of the treasure that I had to guard. I had to look for it and bring it back. Well, then an arrogant old man came to fight me, and in the end we killed each other. Was that my fault? No, of course not!

E My enemies consider themselves great warriors and they say that it is better to avenge a friend's death than to cry for him. Well, I avenged the death of my dear son, and still in their songs they describe me as something horrible, as something grotesque. How strange my enemies are!

F Before coming to the land of the Danes I had lived with the family of one of the most famous murderers in the history of the world! There I lived away from the joy of men near the seas, and so I hated their joy. In the end, though, I too was murdered by a man whose own people had been enemies and murderers of the people I had killed!

G I come from a long line of great kings, and I too was a great king. I rewarded my followers with the treasures we won in war, and I even built, as every great king should, a fantastic mead hall where my men could drink, talk and listen to the stories of great heroes of the past. Still, as every wise man knows, the victories of this earth do not last, and horror came to my land. Fortunately, I lived to see that horror gone forever.

INTERNET PROJECT

Sutton Hoo, the world's greatest Anglo-Saxon burial site

Connect to the Internet and go to www.blackcat-cideb.com or www.cideb.it. Insert the title of the book into our search engine. Open the page for *Beowulf*. Click on the Internet project link. Go down the page until you find the title of this book and click on the relevant links for this project.

Work in small groups and try to discover:

1 who was buried there
2 how many other burial mounds are in this 'cemetery'
3 some of the objects the dead person was buried with
4 when it was discovered
5 what its relationship with *Beowulf* is.

On your own, decide which of the objects you find most beautiful or most interesting. Explain why to the rest of the class.

If you like, you can make comparisons with burial customs in other cultures.

Key to Exit Test

1 **1** D **2** A **3** A **4** C **5** A **6** A **7** C **8** A **9** D **10** B **11** C **12** D

2 Open answer, but include the following ideas.
1 Yes, because the world seems full of dangers, with only a brief moment of safety.
2 Christianity and some other religions try to give meaning to life by teaching that there is something after death. In the story of the little bird there is nothing after death.
3 The mead hall is seen as a place of community and safety.

3 **A** Beowulf **B** Unferth **C** Wiglaf **D** the dragon **E** Grendel's mother **F** Grendel **G** Hrothgar